KU-417-663

Cards on the Table

Agatha Christie is known throughout the world as the Queen of Crime. Her books have sold over a billion copies in English with another billion in 44 foreign languages. She is the most widely published author of all time and in any language, outsold only by the Bible and Shakespeare. She is the author of 80 crime novels and short story collections, 19 plays, and six novels written under the name of Mary Westmacott.

Agatha Christie's first novel, *The Mysterious Affair at Styles*, was written towards the end of the First World War, in which she served as a VAD. In it she created Hercule Poirot, the little Belgian detective who was destined to become the most popular detective in crime fiction since Sherlock Holmes. It was eventually published by The Bodley Head in 1920.

In 1926, after averaging a book a year, Agatha Christie wrote her masterpiece. *The Murder of Roger Ackroyd* was the first of her books to be published by Collins and marked the beginning of an author-publisher relationship which lasted for 50 years and well over 70 books. *The Murder of Roger Ackroyd* was also the first of Agatha Christie's books to be dramatised – under the name *Alibi* – and to have a successful run in London's West End. *The Mousetrap*, her most famous play of all, opened in 1952 and is the longest-running play in history.

Agatha Christie was made a Dame in 1971. She died in 1976, since when a number of books have been published posthumously: the bestselling novel *Sleeping Murder* appeared later that year, followed by her autobiography and the short story collections *Miss Marple's Final Cases*, *Problem at Pollensa Bay* and *While the Light Lasts*. In 1998 *Black Coffee* was the first of her plays to be novelised by another author, Charles Osborne.

BY THE SAME AUTHOR

The ABC Murders
The Adventure of the
  Christmas Pudding
After the Funeral
And Then There Were None
Appointment with Death
At Bertram's Hotel
The Big Four
The Body in the Library
By the Pricking of My Thumbs
Cards on the Table
A Caribbean Mystery
Cat Among the Pigeons
The Clocks
Crooked House
Curtain: Poirot's Last Case
Dead Man's Folly
Death Comes as the End
Death in the Clouds
Death on the Nile
Destination Unknown
Dumb Witness
Elephants Can Remember
Endless Night
Evil Under the Sun
Five Little Pigs
4.50 from Paddington
Hallowe'en Party
Hercule Poirot's Christmas
Hickory Dickory Dock
The Hollow
The Hound of Death
The Labours of Hercules
The Listerdale Mystery
Lord Edgware Dies
The Man in the Brown Suit
The Mirror Crack'd from Side
  to Side
Miss Marple's Final Cases
The Moving Finger
Mrs McGinty's Dead
The Murder at the Vicarage
Murder in Mesopotamia
Murder in the Mews
A Murder is Announced
Murder is Easy
The Murder of Roger Ackroyd
Murder on the Links
Murder on the Orient Express

The Mysterious Affair at Styles
The Mysterious Mr Quin
The Mystery of the Blue Train
Nemesis
N or M?
One, Two, Buckle My Shoe
Ordeal by Innocence
The Pale Horse
Parker Pyne Investigates
Partners in Crime
Passenger to Frankfurt
Peril at End House
A Pocket Full of Rye
Poirot Investigates
Poirot's Early Cases
Postern of Fate
Problem at Pollensa Bay
Sad Cypress
The Secret Adversary
The Secret of Chimneys
The Seven Dials Mystery
The Sittaford Mystery
Sleeping Murder
Sparkling Cyanide
Taken at the Flood
They Came to Baghdad
They Do It With Mirrors
Third Girl
The Thirteen Problems
Three Act Tragedy
Towards Zero
While the Light Lasts
Why Didn't They Ask Evans?

*Novels under the Nom de Plume of
'Mary Westmacott'*
Absent in the Spring
The Burden
A Daughter's a Daughter
Giant's Bread
The Rose and the Yew Tree
Unfinished Portrait

*Books under the name of
Agatha Christie Mallowan*
Come Tell Me How You Live
Star Over Bethlehem

Autobiography
Agatha Christie: An Autobiography

AGATHA CHRISTIE

CARDS ON THE TABLE

HarperCollins*Publishers*

HarperCollins*Publishers*
77-85 Fulham Palace Road,
Hammersmith, London W6 8JB
www.**fire**and**water**.com

This paperback edition 1993
7   9   8

Previously published in paperback by Fontana 1957
Reprinted twenty-three times

First published in Great Britain by
Collins 1936

Copyright Agatha Christie Mallowan 1936

ISBN 0 00 765954 7

Set in Plantin

Printed and bound in Great Britain by
Mackays of Chatham plc, Chatham, Kent

All rights reserved. No part of this publication may be
reproduced, stored in a retrieval system, or transmitted,
in any form or by any means, electronic, mechanical,
photocopying, recording or otherwise, without the prior
permission of the publishers.

This book is sold subject to the condition that it shall not,
by way of trade or otherwise, be lent, re-sold, hired out or
otherwise circulated without the publisher's prior consent
in any form of binding or cover other than that in which it
is published and without a similar condition including this
condition being imposed on the subsequent purchaser.

CONTENTS

FOREWORD BY THE AUTHOR

There is an idea prevalent that a detective story is rather like a big race – a number of starters – likely horses and jockeys. 'You pays your money and you takes your choice!' The favourite is by common consent the opposite of a favourite on the race-course. In other words he is likely to be a complete outsider! Spot the least likely person to have committed the crime and in nine times out of ten your task is finished.

Since I do not want my faithful readers to fling away this book in disgust, I prefer to warn them beforehand *that this is not that kind of book*. There are only *four* starters and any one of them, *given the right circumstances*, might have committed the crime. That knocks out forcibly the element of surprise. Nevertheless there should be, I think, an equal interest attached to four persons, each of whom has committed murder and is capable of committing further murders. They are four widely divergent types, the motive that drives each one of them to crime is peculiar to that person, and each one would employ a different method. The deduction must, therefore, be entirely *psychological*, but it is none the less interesting for that, because when all is said and done it is the *mind* of the murderer that is of supreme interest.

I may say, as an additional argument in favour of this story, that it was one of Hercule Poirot's favourite cases. His friend, Captain Hastings, however, when Poirot described it to him, considered it very dull! I wonder with which of them my readers will agree.

CHAPTER ONE

Mr Shaitana

'My dear M. Poirot!'

It was a soft purring voice – a voice used deliberately as an instrument – nothing impulsive or premeditated about it.

Hercule Poirot swung round.

He bowed.

He shook hands ceremoniously.

There was something in his eye that was unusual. One would have said that this chance encounter awakened in him an emotion that he seldom had occasion to feel.

'My dear Mr Shaitana,' he said.

They both paused. They were like duellists *en garde*.

Around them a well-dressed languid London crowd eddied mildly. Voices drawled or murmured.

'Darling – exquisite!'

'Simply divine, aren't they, my dear?'

It was the Exhibition of Snuff-Boxes at Wessex House. Admission one guinea, in aid of the London hospitals.

'My dear man,' said Mr Shaitana, 'how nice to see you! Not hanging or guillotining much just at present? Slack season in the criminal world? Or is there to be a robbery here this afternoon – that would be too delicious.'

'Alas, Monsieur,' said Poirot. 'I came here in a purely private capacity.'

Mr Shaitana was diverted for a moment by a Lovely Young Thing with tight poodle curls up one side of her head and three cornucopias in black straw on the other.

He said:

'My *dear – why* didn't you come to my party? It really was a marvellous party! Quite a lot of people actually *spoke* to me! One woman even said, "How do you do," and "Goodbye"

9

and "Thank you so much" – but of course she came from a Garden City, poor dear!'

While the Lovely Young Thing made a suitable reply, Poirot allowed himself a good study of the hirsute adornment on Mr Shaitana's upper lip.

A fine moustache – a *very* fine moustache – the only moustache in London, perhaps, that could compete with that of M. Hercule Poirot.

'But it is *not* so luxuriant,' he murmured to himself. 'No, decidedly it is inferior in every respect. *Tout de même*, it catches the eye.'

The whole of Mr Shaitana's person caught the eye – it was designed to do so. He deliberately attempted a Mephistophelian effect. He was tall and thin, his face was long and melancholy, his eyebrows were heavily accented and jet black, he wore a moustache with stiff waxed ends and a tiny black imperial. His clothes were works of art – of exquisite cut – but with a suggestion of bizarre.

Every healthy Englishman who saw him longed earnestly and fervently to kick him! They said, with a singular lack of originality, 'There's that damned Dago, Shaitana!'

Their wives, daughters, sisters, aunts, mothers, and even grandmothers said, varying the idiom according to their generation, words to this effect: 'I know, my dear. Of course, he is *too* terrible. But *so* rich! And such marvellous parties! And he's always got something amusing and spiteful to tell you about people.'

Whether Mr Shaitana was an Argentine, or a Portuguese, or a Greek, or some other nationality rightly despised by the insular Briton, nobody knew.

But three facts were quite certain:

He existed richly and beautifully in a super flat in Park Lane.

He gave wonderful parties – large parties, small parties, *macabre* parties, respectable parties and definitely 'queer' parties.

He was a man of whom nearly everybody was a little afraid.

Why this last was so can hardly be stated in definite words. There was a feeling, perhaps, that he knew a little too much about everybody. And there was a feeling, too, that his sense of humour was a curious one.

People nearly always felt that it would be better not to risk offending Mr Shaitana.

It was his humour this afternoon to bait that ridiculous-looking little man, Hercule Poirot.

'So even a policeman needs recreation?' he said. 'You study the arts in your old age, M. Poirot?'

Poirot smiled good-humouredly.

'I see,' he said, 'that you yourself have lent three snuff-boxes to the Exhibition.'

Mr Shaitana waved a deprecating hand.

'One picks up trifles here and there. You must come to my flat one day. I have some interesting pieces. I do not confine myself to any particular period or class of object.'

'Your tastes are catholic,' said Poirot smiling.

'As you say.'

Suddenly Mr Shaitana's eyes danced, the corners of his lips curled up, his eyebrows assumed a fantastic tilt.

'I could even show you objects in your own line, M. Poirot!'

'You have then a private "Black Museum".'

'Bah!' Mr Shaitana snapped disdainful fingers. 'The cup used by the Brighton murderer, the jemmy of a celebrated burglar – absurd childishness! I should never burden myself with rubbish like that. I collect only the best objects of their kind.'

'And what do you consider the best objects, artistically speaking, in crime?' inquired Poirot.

Mr Shaitana leaned forward and laid two fingers on Poirot's shoulder. He hissed his words dramatically.

'The human beings who commit them, M. Poirot.'

Poirot's eyebrows rose a trifle.

'Aha, I have startled you,' said Mr Shaitana. 'My dear, dear man, you and I look on these things as from poles apart! For you crime is a matter of routine: a murder, an investigation, a clue, and ultimately (for you are undoubtedly an able fellow) a conviction. Such banalities would not interest me! I am not interested in poor specimens of any kind. And the caught murderer is necessarily one of the failures. He is second-rate. No, I look on the matter from the artistic point of view. I collect only the best!'

'The best being – ?' asked Poirot.

'My dear fellow – *the ones who have got away with it!* The successes! The criminals who lead an agreeable life which no breath of suspicion has ever touched. Admit that is an amusing hobby.'

'It was another word I was thinking of – not amusing.'

'An idea!' cried Shaitana, paying no attention to Poirot. 'A little dinner! A dinner to meet my exhibits! Really, that is a most amusing thought. I cannot think why it has never occurred to me before. Yes – yes, I see it exactly . . . You must give me a little time – not next week – let us say the week after next. You are free? What day shall we say?'

'Any day of the week after next would suit me,' said Poirot with a bow.

'Good – then let us say Friday. Friday the 18th, that will be. I will write it down at once in my little book. Really, the idea pleases me enormously.'

'I am not quite sure if it pleases me,' said Poirot slowly. 'I do not mean that I am insensible to the kindness of your invitation – no – not that –'

Shaitana interrupted him.

'But it shocks your *bourgeois* sensibilities? My dear fellow, you *must* free yourself from the limitations of the policeman mentality.'

Poirot said slowly:

'It is true that I have a thoroughly *bourgeois* attitude to murder.'

'But, my dear, *why*? A stupid, bungled, butchering business – yes, I agree with you. But murder can be an *art*! A murderer can be an artist.'

'Oh, I admit it.'

'Well then?' Mr Shaitana asked.

'But he is still a murderer!'

'Surely, my dear M. Poirot, to do a thing supremely well is a *justification*! You want, very unimaginatively, to take every murderer, handcuff him, shut him up, and eventually break his neck for him in the early hours of the morning. In my opinion a really successful murderer should be granted a pension out of the public funds and asked out to dinner!'

Poirot shrugged his shoulders.

'I am not as insensitive to art in crime as you think. I can admire the perfect murder – I can also admire a tiger – that splendid tawny-striped beast. But I will admire him from outside his cage. I will not go inside. That is to say, not unless it is my duty to do so. For you see, Mr Shaitana, the tiger might spring . . .'

Mr Shaitana laughed.

'I see. And the murderer?'

'Might murder,' said Poirot gravely.

'My dear fellow – what an alarmist you are! Then you will not come to meet my collection of – tigers?'

'On the contrary, I shall be enchanted.'

'How brave!'

'You do not quite understand me, Mr Shaitana. My words were in the nature of a warning. You asked me just now to admit that your idea of a collection of murderers was amusing. I said I could think of another word other than amusing. That word was dangerous. I fancy, Mr Shaitana, that your hobby might be a dangerous one!'

Mr Shaitana laughed, a very Mephistophelian laugh.

He said:

'I may expect you, then, on the 18th?'

Poirot gave a little bow.

'You may expect me on the 18th. *Mille remerciments.*'

'I shall arrange a little party,' mused Shaitana. 'Do not forget. Eight o'clock.'

He moved away. Poirot stood a minute or two looking after him.

He shook his head slowly and thoughtfully.

CHAPTER TWO

Dinner at Mr Shaitana's

The door of Mr Shaitana's flat opened noiselessly. A grey-haired butler drew it back to let Poirot enter. He closed it equally noiselessly and deftly relieved the guest of his overcoat and hat.

He murmured in a low expressionless voice:

'What name shall I say?'

'M. Hercule Poirot.'

There was a little hum of talk that eddied out into the hall as the butler opened a door and announced:

'M. Hercule Poirot.'

Sherry-glass in hand, Shaitana came forward to meet him. He was, as usual, immaculately dressed. The Mephistophelian suggestion was heightened tonight, the eyebrows seemed accentuated in their mocking twist.

'Let me introduce you – do you know Mrs Oliver?'

The showman in him enjoyed the little start of surprise that Poirot gave.

Mrs Ariadne Oliver was extremely well-known as one of the foremost writers of detective and other sensational stories. She wrote chatty (if not particularly grammatical) articles on *The Tendency of the Criminal; Famous Crimes Passionnels; Murder for Love v. Murder for Gain.* She was also a hot-headed feminist, and when any murder of importance was occupying space in the Press there was sure to be an interview with Mrs Oliver, and it was mentioned that Mrs Oliver had said, 'Now if a *woman* were the head of Scotland Yard!' She was an earnest believer in woman's intuition.

For the rest she was an agreeable woman of middle age, handsome in a rather untidy fashion with fine eyes, substantial shoulders and a large quantity of rebellious grey hair with which she was continually experimenting. One day her appearance would be highly intellectual – a brow with the hair scraped back from it and coiled in a large bun in the neck – on another Mrs Oliver would suddenly appear with Madonna loops, or large masses of slightly untidy curls. On this particular evening Mrs Oliver was trying out a fringe.

She greeted Poirot, whom she had met before at a literary dinner, in an agreeable bass voice.

'And Superintendent Battle you doubtless know,' said Mr Shaitana.

A big, square, wooden-faced man moved forward. Not only did an onlooker feel that Superintendent Battle was carved out of wood – he also managed to convey the impression that the wood in question was the timber out of a battleship.

Superintendent Battle was supposed to be Scotland Yard's best representative. He always looked stolid and rather stupid.

'I know M. Poirot,' said Superintendent Battle.

And his wooden face creased into a smile and then returned to its former unexpressiveness.

'Colonel Race,' went on Mr Shaitana.

Poirot had not previously met Colonel Race, but he knew something about him. A dark, handsome, deeply bronzed man of fifty, he was usually to be found in some outpost of empire – especially if there were trouble brewing. Secret Service is a melodramatic term, but it described pretty accurately to the lay mind the nature and scope of Colonel Race's activities.

Poirot had by now taken in and appreciated the particular essence of his host's humorous intentions.

'Our other guests are late,' said Mr Shaitana. 'My fault, perhaps. I believe I told them 8.15.'

But at that moment the door opened and the butler announced:

'Dr Roberts.'

The man who came in did so with a kind of parody of a brisk bedside manner. He was a cheerful, highly-coloured individual of middle age. Small twinkling eyes, a touch of baldness, a tendency to *embonpoint* and a general air of well-scrubbed and disinfected medical practitioner. His manner was cheerful and confident. You felt that his diagnosis would be correct and his treatments agreeable and practical – 'a little champagne in convalescence perhaps.' A man of the world!

'Not late, I hope?' said Dr Roberts genially.

He shook hands with his host and was introduced to the others. He seemed particularly gratified at meeting Battle.

'Why, you're one of the big noises at Scotland Yard, aren't you? This *is* interesting! Too bad to make you talk shop but I warn you I shall have a try at it. Always been interested in crime. Bad thing for a doctor, perhaps. Mustn't say so to my nervous patients – ha ha!'

Again the door opened.

'Mrs Lorrimer.'

Mrs Lorrimer was a well-dressed woman of sixty. She had finely-cut features, beautifully arranged grey hair, and a clear, incisive voice.

'I hope I'm not late,' she said, advancing to her host.

She turned from him to greet Dr Roberts, with whom she was acquainted.

The butler announced:

'Major Despard.'

Major Despard was a tall, lean, handsome man, his face slightly marred by a scar on the temple. Introductions completed, he gravitated naturally to the side of Colonel Race – and the two men were soon talking sport and comparing their experiences on *safari*.

For the last time the door opened and the butler announced:

17

'Miss Meredith.'

A girl in the early twenties entered. She was of medium height and pretty. Brown curls clustered in her neck, her grey eyes were large and wide apart. Her face was powdered but not made up. Her voice was slow and rather shy.

She said:

'Oh dear, am I the last?'

Mr Shaitana descended on her with sherry and an ornate and complimentary reply. His introductions were formal and almost ceremonious.

Miss Meredith was left sipping her sherry by Poirot's side.

'Our friend is very punctilious,' said Poirot with a smile.

The girl agreed.

'I know. People rather dispense with introductions nowadays. They just say "I expect you know everybody" and leave it at that.'

'Whether you do or you don't?'

'Whether you do or don't. Sometimes it makes it awkward – but I think this is more awe-inspiring.'

She hesitated and then said:

'Is that Mrs Oliver, the novelist?'

Mrs Oliver's bass voice rose powerfully at that minute, speaking to Dr Roberts.

'You can't get away from a woman's instinct, doctor. Women know these things.'

Forgetting that she no longer had a brow she endeavoured to sweep her hair back from it but was foiled by the fringe.

'That is Mrs Oliver,' said Poirot.

'The one who wrote *The Body in the Library*?'

'That identical one.'

Miss Meredith frowned a little.

'And that wooden-looking man – a *superintendent* did Mr Shaitana say?'

'From Scotland Yard.'

'And you?'

'And me?'

'I know all about you, M. Poirot. It was you who really solved the A.B.C. crimes.'

'Madamoiselle, you cover me with confusion.'

Miss Meredith drew her brows together.

'Mr Shaitana,' she began and then stopped. 'Mr Shaitana –'

Poirot said quietly:

'One might say he was "crime-minded". It seems so. Doubtless he wishes to hear us dispute ourselves. He is already egging on Mrs Oliver and Dr Roberts. They are now discussing untraceable poisons.'

Miss Meredith gave a little gasp as she said:

'What a queer man he is!'

'Dr Roberts?'

'No, Mr Shaitana.'

She shivered a little and said:

'There's always something a little frightening about him, I think. You never know what would strike him as amusing. It might – it might be something *cruel*.'

'Such as fox-hunting, eh?'

Miss Meredith threw him a reproachful glance.

'I meant – oh! something *Oriental*!'

'He has perhaps the tortuous mind,' admitted Poirot.

'Torturer's?'

'No, no tortuous, I said.'

'I don't think I like him frightfully,' confided Miss Meredith, her voice dropping.

'You will like his dinner, though,' Poirot assured her. 'He has a marvellous cook.'

She looked at him doubtfully and then laughed.

'Why,' she exclaimed, 'I believe you are quite human.'

'But certainly I am human!'

'You see,' said Miss Meredith, 'all these celebrities are rather intimidating.'

'Mademoiselle, you should not be intimidated – you should be thrilled! You should have all ready your autograph book and your fountain-pen.'

'Well, you see, I'm not really terribly interested in crime. I don't think women are: it's always men who read detective stories.'

Hercule Poirot sighed affectedly.

'Alas!' he murmured. 'What would I not give at this minute to be even the most minor of film stars!'

The butler threw the door open.

'Dinner is served,' he murmured.

Poirot's prognostication was amply justified. The dinner was delicious and its serving perfection. Subdued light, polished wood, the blue gleam of Irish glass. In the dimness, at the head of the table, Mr Shaitana looked more than ever diabolical.

He apologized gracefully for the uneven number of the sexes.

Mrs Lorrimer was on his right hand, Mrs Oliver on his left. Miss Meredith was between Superintendent Battle and Major Despard. Poirot was between Mrs Lorrimer and Dr Roberts.

The latter murmured facetiously to him.

'You're not going to be allowed to monopolize the only pretty girl all the evening. You French fellows, you don't waste your time, do you?'

'I happen to be Belgian,' murmured Poirot.

'Same thing where the ladies are concerned, I expect, my boy,' said the doctor cheerfully.

Then, dropping the facetiousness, and adopting a professional tone, he began to talk to Colonel Race on his other side about the latest developments in the treatment of sleeping sickness.

Mrs Lorrimer turned to Poirot and began to talk of the latest plays. Her judgements were sound and her criticisms apt. They drifted on to books and then to world politics. He found her a well-informed and thoroughly intelligent woman.

On the opposite side of the table Mrs Oliver was asking Major Despard if he knew of any unheard-of out-of-the-way poisons.

'Well, there's *curare*.'

'My *dear* man, *vieux jeu*! That's been done hundreds of times. I mean something *new*!'

Major Despard said drily:

'Primitive tribes are rather old-fashioned. They stick to the good old stuff their grandfathers and great-grandfathers used before them.'

'Very tiresome of them,' said Mrs Oliver. 'I should have thought they were always experimenting with pounding up herbs and things. Such a chance for explorers, I always think. They could come home and kill off all their rich old uncles with some new drug that no one's ever heard of.'

'You should go to civilization, not to the wilds for that,' said Despard. 'In the modern laboratory, for instance. Cultures of innocent-looking germs that will produce bona fide diseases.'

'That wouldn't do for *my* public,' said Mrs Oliver. 'Besides one is so apt to get the names wrong – staphylococcus and streptococcus and all those things – so difficult for my secretary and anyway rather dull, don't you think so? What do *you* think, Superintendent Battle?'

'In real life people don't bother about being too subtle, Mrs Oliver,' said the superintendent. 'They usually stick to arsenic because it's nice and handy to get hold of.'

'Nonsense,' said Mrs Oliver. 'That's simply because there are lots of crimes you people at Scotland Yard never find out. Now if you had a woman there –'

'As a matter of fact we have –'

'Yes, those dreadful policewomen in funny hats who bother people in parks! I mean a woman at the head of things. Women *know* about crime.'

'They're usually very successful criminals,' said Superintendent Battle. 'Keep their heads well. It's amazing how they'll brazen things out.'

Mr Shaitana laughed gently.

'Poison is a woman's weapon,' he said. 'There must be many secret women poisoners – never found out.'

'Of course there are,' said Mrs Oliver happily, helping herself lavishly to a *mousse* of *foie gras*.

'A doctor, too, has opportunities,' went on Mr Shaitana thoughtfully.

'I protest,' cried Dr Roberts. 'When we poison our patients it's entirely by accident.' He laughed heartily.

'But if I were to commit a crime,' went on Mr Shaitana.

He stopped, and something in that pause compelled attention.

All faces were turned to him.

'I should make it very simple, I think. There's always an accident – a shooting accident, for instance – or the domestic kind of accident.'

Then he shrugged his shoulders and picked up his wine-glass.

'But who am I to pronounce – with so many experts present . . .'

He drank. The candlelight threw a red shade from the wine on to his face with its waxed moustache, its little imperial, its fantastic eyebrows . . .

There was a momentary silence.

Mrs Oliver said:

'Is it twenty-to or twenty-past? An angel passing . . . My feet aren't crossed – it must be a black angel!'

CHAPTER THREE

A Game of Bridge

When the company returned to the drawing-room a bridge table had been set out. Coffee was handed round.

'Who plays bridge?' asked Mr Shaitana. 'Mrs Lorrimer, I know. And Dr Roberts. Do you play, Miss Meredith?'

'Yes. I'm not frightfully good, though.'

'Excellent. And Major Despard? Good. Supposing you four play here.'

'Thank goodness there's to be bridge,' said Mrs Lorrimer in an aside to Poirot. 'I'm one of the worst bridge fiends that ever lived. It's growing on me. I simply will *not* go out to dinner now if there's no bridge afterwards! I just fall asleep. I'm ashamed of myself, but there it is.'

They cut for partners. Mrs Lorrimer was partnered with Anne Meredith against Major Despard and Dr Roberts.

'Women against men,' said Mrs Lorrimer as she took her seat and began shuffling the cards in an expert manner. 'The blue cards, don't you think, partner? I'm a forcing two.'

'Mind you win,' said Mrs Oliver, her feminist feelings rising. 'Show the men they can't have it all their own way.'

'They haven't got a hope, the poor dears,' said Dr Roberts cheerfully as he started shuffling the other pack. 'Your deal, I think, Mrs Lorrimer.'

Major Despard sat down rather slowly. He was looking at Anne Meredith as though he had just made the discovery that she was remarkably pretty.

'Cut, please,' said Mrs Lorrimer impatiently. And with a start of apology he cut the pack she was presenting to him.

Mrs Lorrimer began to deal with a practised hand.

'There is another bridge table in the other room,' said Mr Shaitana.

He crossed to a second door and the other four followed him into a small comfortably furnished smoking-room where a second bridge table was set ready.

'We must cut out,' said Colonel Race.

Mr Shaitana shook his head.

'I do not play,' he said. 'Bridge is not one of the games that amuse me.'

The others protested that they would much rather not play, but he overruled them firmly and in the end they sat down. Poirot and Mrs Oliver against Battle and Race.

Mr Shaitana watched them for a little while, smiled in a Mephistophelian manner as he observed on what hand Mrs Oliver declared Two No Trumps, and then went noiselessly through into the other room.

There they were well down to it, their faces serious, the bids coming quickly. 'One heart.' 'Pass.' 'Three clubs.' 'Three spades.' 'Four diamonds.' 'Double.' 'Four hearts.'

Mr Shaitana stood watching a moment, smiling to himself.

Then he crossed the room and sat down in a big chair by the fireplace. A tray of drinks had been brought in and placed on an adjacent table. The firelight gleamed on the crystal stoppers.

Always an artist in lighting, Mr Shaitana had simulated the appearance of a merely firelit room. A small shaded lamp at his elbow gave him light to read by if he so desired. Discreet floodlighting gave the room a subdued look. A slightly stronger light shone over the bridge table, from whence the monotonous ejaculations continued.

'One no trump' – clear and decisive – Mrs Lorrimer.

'Three hearts' – an aggressive note in the voice – Dr Roberts.

'No bid' – a quiet voice – Anne Meredith's.

A slight pause always before Despard's voice came. Not so much a slow thinker as a man who liked to be sure before he spoke.

'Four hearts.'

'Double.'

His face lit up by the flickering firelight, Mr Shaitana smiled.

He smiled and he went on smiling. His eyelids flickered a little . . .

His party was amusing him.

'Five diamonds. Game and rubber,' said Colonel Race. 'Good for you, partner,' he said to Poirot. 'I didn't think you'd do it. Lucky they didn't lead a spade.'

'Wouldn't have made much difference, I expect,' said Superintendent Battle, a man of gentle magnanimity.

He had called spades. His partner, Mrs Oliver, had had a spade, but 'something had told her' to lead a club – with disastrous results.

Colonel Race looked at his watch.

'Ten-past-twelve. Time for another?'

'You'll excuse me,' said Superintendent Battle. 'But I'm by way of being an "early-to-bed" man.'

'I, too,' said Hercule Poirot.

'We'd better add up,' said Race.

The result of the evening's five rubbers was an overwhelming victory for the male sex. Mrs Oliver had lost three pounds and seven shillings to the other three. The biggest winner was Colonel Race.

Mrs Oliver, though a bad bridge player, was a sporting loser. She paid up cheerfully.

'Everything went wrong for me tonight,' she said. 'It is like that sometimes. I held the most beautiful cards yesterday. A hundred and fifty honours three times running.'

She rose and gathered up her embroidered evening bag, just refraining in time from stroking her hair off her brow.

'I suppose our host is next door,' she said.

She went through the communicating door, the others behind her.

Mr Shaitana was in his chair by the fire. The bridge players were absorbed in their game.

'Double five clubs,' Mrs Lorrimer was saying in her cool, incisive voice.

'Five No Trumps.'

'Double five No Trumps.'

Mrs Oliver came up to the bridge table. This was likely to be an exciting hand.

Superintendent Battle came with her.

Colonel Race went towards Mr Shaitana, Poirot behind him.

'Got to be going, Shaitana,' said Race.

Mr Shaitana did not answer. His head had fallen forward, and he seemed to be asleep. Race gave a momentary whimsical glance at Poirot and went a little nearer. Suddenly he uttered a muffled exclamation, bent forward. Poirot was beside him in a minute, he, too, looking where Colonel Race was pointing – something that might have been a particularly ornate shirt stud – but was not . . .

Poirot bent, raised one of Mr Shaitana's hands, then let it fall. He met Race's inquiring glance and nodded. The latter raised his voice.

'Superintendent Battle, just a minute.'

The superintendent came over to them. Mrs Oliver continued to watch the play of Five No Trumps doubled.

Superintendent Battle, despite his appearance of stolidity, was a very quick man. His eyebrows went up and he said in a low voice as he joined them:

'Something wrong?'

With a nod Colonel Race indicated the silent figure in the chair.

As Battle bent over it, Poirot looked thoughtfully at what he could see of Mr Shaitana's face. Rather a silly face it looked now, the mouth drooping open – the devilish expression lacking . . .

Hercule Poirot shook his head.

Superintendent Battle straightened himself. He had examined, without touching, the thing which looked like an extra stud in Mr Shaitana's shirt – and it was not an extra stud. He had raised the limp hand and let it fall.

Now he stood up, unemotional, capable, soldierly – prepared to take charge efficiently of the situation.

'Just a minute, please,' he said.

And the raised voice was his official voice, so different that all the heads at the bridge table turned to him, and Anne Meredith's hand remained poised over an ace of spades in dummy.

'I'm sorry to tell you all,' he said, 'that our host, Mr Shaitana, is dead.'

Mrs Lorrimer and Dr Roberts rose to their feet. Despard stared and frowned. Anne Meredith gave a little gasp.

'Are you sure, man?'

Dr Roberts, his professional instincts aroused, came briskly across the floor with a bounding medical 'in-at-the-death' step.

Without seeming to, the bulk of Superintendent Battle impeded his progress.

'Just a minute, Dr Roberts. Can you tell me first who's been in and out of this room this evening?'

Roberts stared at him.

'In and out? I don't understand you. Nobody has.'

The superintendent transferred his gaze.

'Is that right, Mrs Lorrimer?'

'Quite right.'

'Not the butler nor any of the servants?'

'No. The butler brought in that tray as we sat down to bridge. He has not been in since.'

Superintendent Battle looked at Despard.

Despard nodded in agreement.

Anne said rather breathlessly, 'Yes – yes, that's right.'

'What's all this, man,' said Roberts impatiently. 'Just let me examine him; may be just a fainting fit.'

'It isn't a fainting fit, and I'm sorry – *but nobody's going to touch him until the divisional surgeon comes. Mr Shaitana's been murdered, ladies and gentlemen.*'

'Murdered?' A horrified incredulous sigh from Anne.

A stare – a very blank stare – from Despard.

A sharp incisive 'Murdered?' from Mrs Lorrimer.

A 'Good God!' from Dr Roberts.

Superintendent Battle nodded his head slowly. He looked rather like a Chinese porcelain mandarin. His expression was quite blank.

'Stabbed,' he said. 'That's the way of it. Stabbed.'

Then he shot out a question:

'Any of you leave the bridge table during the evening?'

He saw four expressions break up – waver. He saw fear – comprehension – indignation – dismay – horror; but he saw nothing definitely helpful.

'Well?'

There was a pause, and then Major Despard said quietly (he had risen now and was standing like a soldier on parade, his narrow, intelligent face turned to Battle):

'I think every one of us, at one time or another, moved from the bridge table – either to get drinks or to put wood on the fire. I did both. When I went to the fire Shaitana was asleep in the chair.'

'Asleep?'

'I thought so – yes.'

'He may have been,' said Battle. 'Or he may have been dead then. We'll go into that presently. I'll ask you now to go into the room next door.' He turned to the quiet figure at his elbow: 'Colonel Race, perhaps you'll go with them?'

Race gave a quick nod of comprehension.

'Right, Superintendent.'

The four bridge players went slowly through the doorway.

Mrs Oliver sat down in a chair at the far end of the room and began to sob quietly.

Battle took up the telephone receiver and spoke. Then he said:

'The local police will be round immediately. Orders from headquarters are that I'm to take on the case. Divisional surgeon will be here almost at once. How long should you say he'd been dead, M. Poirot? I'd say well over an hour myself.'

'I agree. Alas, that one cannot be more exact – that one cannot say, "This man has been dead one hour, twenty-five minutes and forty seconds."'

Battle nodded absently.

'He was sitting right in front of the fire. That makes a slight difference. Over an hour – not more than two and a half: that's what our doctor will say, I'll be bound. And nobody heard anything and nobody saw anything. Amazing! What a desperate chance to take. He might have cried out.'

'But he did not. The murderer's luck held. As you say, *mon ami*, it was a very desperate business.'

'Any idea, M. Poirot, as to motive? Anything of that kind?'

Poirot said slowly:

'Yes, I have something to say on that score. Tell me, M. Shaitana – he did not give you any hint of what kind of a party you were coming to tonight?'

Superintendent Battle looked at him curiously.

'No, M. Poirot. He didn't say anything at all. Why?'

A bell whirred in the distance and a knocker was plied.

'That's our people,' said Superintendent Battle. 'I'll go and let 'em in. We'll have your story presently. Must get on with the routine work.'

Poirot nodded.

Battle left the room.

Mrs Oliver continued to sob.

Poirot went over to the bridge table. Without touching anything, he examined the scores. He shook his head once or twice.

'The stupid little man! Oh, the stupid little man,' murmured Hercule Poirot. 'To dress up as the devil and try to frighten people. *Quel enfantillage!*'

The door opened. The divisional surgeon came in, bag in hand. He was followed by the divisional inspector, talking to Battle. A camera man came next. There was a constable in the hall.

The routine of the detection of crime had begun.

CHAPTER FOUR

First Murderer?

Hercule Poirot, Mrs Oliver, Colonel Race and Superintendent Battle sat round the dining-room table.

It was an hour later. The body had been examined, photographed and removed. A fingerprint expert had been and gone.

Superintendent Battle looked at Poirot.

'Before I have those four in, I want to hear what you've got to tell me. According to you there was something behind this party tonight?'

Very deliberately and carefully Poirot retold the conversation he had held with Shaitana at Wessex House.

Superintendent Battle pursed his lips. He very nearly whistled.

'Exhibits – eh? Murderers all alive oh! And you think he *meant* it? You don't think he was pulling your leg?'

Poirot shook his head.

'Oh, no, he meant it. Shaitana was a man who prided himself on his Mephistophelian attitude to life. He was a man of great vanity. He was also a stupid man – that is why he is dead.'

'I get you,' said Superintendent Battle, following things out in his mind. 'A party of eight and himself. Four "sleuths", so to speak – and four murderers!'

'It's impossible!' cried Mrs Oliver. 'Absolutely impossible. None of those people can be *criminals*.'

Superintendent Battle shook his head thoughtfully.

'I wouldn't be so sure of that, Mrs Oliver. Murderers look and behave very much like everybody else. Nice, quiet, well-behaved, reasonable folk very often.'

'In that case, it's Dr Roberts,' said Mrs Oliver firmly. 'I

felt instinctively that there was something wrong with that man as soon as I saw him. My instincts never lie.'

Battle turned to Colonel Race.

Race shrugged his shoulders. He took the question as referring to Poirot's statment and not to Mrs Oliver's suspicions.

'It could be,' he said. 'It could be. It shows that Shaitana was right in *one* case at least! After all, he can only have *suspected* that these people were murderers – he can't have been *sure*. He may have been right in all four cases, he may have been right in only one case – but he was right in *one* case; his death proved that.'

'One of them got the wind up. Think that's it, M. Poirot?'

Poirot nodded.

'The late Mr Shaitana had a reputation,' he said. 'He had a dangerous sense of humour, and was reputed to be merciless. The victim thought that Shaitana was giving himself an evening's amusement, leading up to a moment when he'd hand the victim over to the police – *you*! He (or she) must have thought that Shaitana had definite evidence.'

'Had he?'

Poirot shrugged his shoulders.

'That we shall never know.'

'Dr Roberts!' repeated Mrs Oliver firmly. 'Such a hearty man. Murderers are often hearty – as a disguise! If I were you, Superintendent Battle, I should arrest him at once.'

'I dare say we would if there was a Woman at the Head of Scotland Yard,' said Superintendent Battle, a momentary twinkle showing in his unemotional eye. 'But, you see, mere men being in charge, we've got to be careful. We've got to get there slowly.'

'Oh, men – men,' sighed Mrs Oliver, and began to compose newspaper articles in her head.

'Better have them in now,' said Superintendent Battle. 'It won't do to keep them hanging about too long.'

Colonel Race half rose.

'If you'd like us to go –'

Superintendent Battle hesitated a minute as he caught Mrs Oliver's eloquent eye. He was well aware of Colonel Race's official position, and Poirot had worked with the police on many occasions. For Mrs Oliver to remain was decidedly stretching a point. But Battle was a kindly man. He remembered that Mrs Oliver had lost three pounds and seven shillings at bridge, and that she had been a cheerful loser.

'You can all stay,' he said, 'as far as I'm concerned. But no interruptions, please (he looked at Mrs Oliver), and there mustn't be a hint of what M. Poirot had just told us. That was Shaitana's little secret, and to all intents and purposes it died with him. Understand?'

'Perfectly,' said Mrs Oliver.

Battle strode to the door and called the constable who was on duty in the hall.

'Go to the little smoking-room. You'll find Anderson there with four guests. Ask Dr Roberts if he'll be so good as to step this way.'

'I should have kept him to the end,' said Mrs Oliver. 'In a book, I mean,' she added apologetically.

'Real life's a bit different,' said Battle.

'I know,' said Mrs Oliver. 'Badly constructed.'

Dr Roberts entered with the springiness of his step slightly subdued.

'I say, Battle,' he said. 'This is the devil of a business! Excuse me, Mrs Oliver, but it is. Professionally speaking, I could hardly have believed it! To stab a man with three other people a few yards away.' He shook his head. 'Whew! I wouldn't like to have done it!' A slight smile twitched up the corners of his mouth. 'What can I say or do to convince you that I *didn't* do it?'

'Well, there's motive, Dr Roberts.'

The doctor nodded his head emphatically.

'That's all clear. I hadn't the shadow of a motive for doing away with poor Shaitana. I didn't even know him very well. He amused me – he was such a fantastic fellow. Touch of the Oriental about him. Naturally, you'll investigate my relations with him closely – I expect that. I'm not a fool. But you won't find anything. I'd no reason for killing Shaitana, and I didn't kill him.'

Superintendent Battle nodded woodenly.

'That's all right, Dr Roberts. I've got to investigate as you know. You're a sensible man. Now, can you tell me anything about the other three people?'

'I'm afraid I don't know very much. Despard and Miss Meredith I met for the first time tonight. I knew of Despard before – read his travel book, and a jolly good yarn it is.'

'Did you know that he and Mr Shaitana were acquainted?'

'No. Shaitana never mentioned him to me. As I say, I'd heard of him, but never met him. Miss Meredith I've never seen before. Mrs Lorrimer I know slightly.'

'What do you know about her?'

Roberts shrugged his shoulders.

'She's a widow. Moderately well off. Intelligent, well-bred woman – first-class bridge player. That's where I've met her, as a matter of fact – playing bridge.'

'And Mr Shaitana never mentioned her, either?'

'No.'

'H'm – that doesn't help us much. Now, Dr Roberts, perhaps you'll be so kind as to tax your memory carefully and tell me how often you yourself left your seat at the bridge table, and all you can remember about the movements of the others.'

Dr Roberts took a few minutes to think.

'It's difficult,' he said frankly. 'I can remember my own movements, more or less. I got up three times – that is, on three occasions when I was dummy I left my seat and made myself useful. Once I went over and put wood on the fire. Once I brought drinks to the two ladies. Once I poured out a whisky and soda for myself.'

'Can you remember the times?'

'I could only say very roughly. We began to play about nine-thirty, I imagine. I should say it was about an hour later that I stoked the fire, quite a short time after that I fetched the drinks (next hand but one, I think), and perhaps half-past eleven when I got myself a whisky and soda – but those times are quite approximate. I couldn't answer for their being correct.'

'The table with the drinks was beyond Mr Shaitana's chair?'

'Yes. That's to say, I passed quite near him three times.'

'And each time, to the best of your belief, he was asleep?'

'That's what I thought the first time. The second time I didn't even look at him. Third time I rather fancy the thought just passed through my mind: "How the beggar does sleep." But I didn't really look closely at him.'

'Very good. Now, when did your fellow-players leave their seats?'

Dr Roberts frowned.

'Difficult – very difficult. Despard went and fetched an extra ash-tray, I think. And he went for a drink. That was before me, for I remember he asked me if I'd have one, and I said I wasn't quite ready.'

'And the ladies?'

'Mrs Lorrimer went over to the fire once. Poked it, I think. I rather fancy she spoke to Shaitana, but I don't know. I was playing a rather tricky no trump at the time.'

'And Miss Meredith?'

'She certainly left the table once. Came round and looked at my hand – I was her partner at the time. Then she looked at the other people's hands, and then she wandered round the room. I don't know what she was doing exactly. I wasn't paying attention.'

Superintendent Battle said thoughtfully:

'As you were sitting at the bridge table, no one's chair was directly facing the fireplace?'

'No, sort of sideways on, and there was a big cabinet between – Chinese piece, very handsome. I can see, of course, that it would be perfectly *possible* to stab the old boy. After all, when you're playing bridge, you're playing bridge. You're not looking round you, and noticing what is going on. The only person who's likely to be doing that is dummy. And in this case –'

'In this case, undoubtedly, dummy was the murderer,' said Superintendent Battle.

'All the same,' said Dr Roberts, 'it wanted nerve, you know. After all, who is to say that somebody won't look up just at the critical moment?'

'Yes,' said Battle. 'It was a big risk. The motive must have been a strong one. I wish we knew what it was,' he added with unblushing mendacity.

'You'll find out, I expect,' said Roberts. 'You'll go through his papers, and all that sort of thing. There will probably be a clue.'

'We'll hope so,' said Superintendent Battle gloomily.

He shot a keen glance at the other.

'I wonder if you'd oblige me, Dr Roberts, by giving me a personal opinion – as man to man.'

'Certainly.'

'Which do you fancy yourself of the three?'

Dr Roberts shrugged his shoulders.

'That's easy. Off-hand, I'd say Despard. The man's got plenty of nerve; he's used to a dangerous life where you've got to act quickly. He wouldn't mind taking a risk. It doesn't seem to me likely the women are in on this. Take a bit of strength, I should imagine.'

'Not so much as you might think. Take a look at this.'

Rather like a conjurer, Battle suddenly produced a long thin instrument of gleaming metal with a small round jewelled head.

Dr Roberts leaned forward, took it, and examined it with rich professional appreciation. He tried the point and whistled.

'What a tool! What a tool! Absolutely made for murder, this little boy. Go in like butter – absolutely like butter. Brought it with him, I suppose.'

'No. It was Mr Shaitana's. It lay on the table near the door with a good many other knick-knacks.'

'So the murderer helped himself. A bit of luck finding a tool like that.'

'Well, that's one way of looking at it,' said Battle slowly.

'Well, of course, it wasn't luck for Shaitana, poor fellow.'

'I didn't mean that, Dr Roberts. I meant that there was another angle of looking at the business. It occurs to me that it was noticing this weapon that put the idea of murder into our criminal's mind.'

'You mean it was a sudden inspiration – that the murder wasn't premeditated? He conceived the idea after he got here? Er – anything to suggest that idea to you?'

He glanced at him searchingly.

'It's just an idea,' said Superintendent Battle stolidly.

'Well, it might be so, of course,' said Dr Roberts slowly.

Superintendent Battle cleared his throat.

'Well, I won't keep you any longer, doctor. Thank you for your help. Perhaps you'll leave your address.'

'Certainly. 200 Gloucester Terrace, W. 2. Telephone No. Bayswater 23896.'

'Thank you. I may have to call upon you shortly.'

'Delighted to see you any time. Hope there won't be too much in the papers. I don't want my nervous patients upset.'

Superintendent Battle looked round at Poirot.

'Excuse me, M. Poirot. If you'd like to ask any questions, I'm sure the doctor wouldn't mind.'

'Of course not. Of course not. Great admirer of yours, M. Poirot. Little grey cells – order and method. I know all about it. I feel sure you'll think of something most intriguing to ask me.'

Hercule Poirot spread out his hands in his most foreign manner.

'No, no. I just like to get all the details clear in my mind. For instance, how many rubbers did you play?'

'Three,' said Roberts promptly. 'We'd got to one game all, in the fourth rubber, when you came in.'

'And who played with who?'

'First rubber, Despard and I against the ladies. They beat us, God bless 'em. Walk over; we never held a card.

'Second rubber, Miss Meredith and I against Despard and Mrs Lorrimer. Third rubber, Mrs Lorrimer and I against Miss Meredith and Despard. We cut each time, but it worked out like a pivot. Fourth rubber, Miss Meredith and I again.'

'Who won and who lost?'

'Mrs Lorrimer won every rubber. Miss Meredith won the first and lost the next two. I was a bit up and Miss Meredith and Despard must have been down.'

Poirot said, smiling, 'The good superintendent has asked you your opinion of your companions as candidates for murder. I now ask you for your opinion of them as bridge players.'

'Mrs Lorrimer's first class,' Dr Roberts replied promptly. 'I'll bet she makes a good income a year out of bridge. Despard's a good player, too – what I call a *sound* player – long-headed chap. Miss Meredith you might describe as quite a safe player. She doesn't make mistakes, but she isn't brilliant.'

'And you yourself, doctor?'

Roberts' eyes twinkled.

'I overcall my hand a bit, or so they say. But I've always found it pays.'

Poirot smiled.

Dr Roberts rose.

'Anything more?'

Poirot shook his head.

'Well, goodnight, then. Goodnight, Mrs Oliver. You ought to get some copy out of this. Better than your untraceable poisons, eh?'

Dr Roberts left the room, his bearing springy once more. Mrs Oliver said bitterly as the door closed behind him:

'Copy! Copy indeed! People are so unintelligent. I could invent a better murder *any* day than anything *real*. I'm *never* at a loss for a plot. And the people who read my books *like* untraceable poisons!'

CHAPTER FIVE

Second Murderer?

Mrs Lorrimer came into the dining-room like a gentle-woman. She looked a little pale, but composed.

'I'm sorry to have to bother you,' Superintendent Battle began.

'You must do your duty, of course,' said Mrs Lorrimer quietly. 'It is, I agree, an unpleasant position in which to be placed, but there is no good shirking it. I quite realize that one of the four people in that room must be guilty. Naturally, I can't expect you to take my word that I am not the person.'

She accepted the chair that Colonel Race offered her and sat down opposite the superintendent. Her intelligent grey eyes met his. She waited attentively.

'You knew Mr Shaitana well?' began the superintendent.

'Not very well. I have known him over a period of some years, but never intimately.'

'Where did you meet him?'

'At a hotel in Egypt — the Winter Palace at Luxor, I think.'

'What did you think of him?'

Mrs Lorrimer shrugged her shoulders slightly.

'I thought him — I may as well say so — rather a charlatan.'

'You had — excuse me for asking — no motive for wishing him out of the way?'

Mrs Lorrimer looked slightly amused.

'Really, Superintendent Battle, do you think I should admit it if I had?'

'You might,' said Battle. 'A really intelligent person might know that a thing was bound to come out.'

Mrs Lorrimer inclined her head thoughtfully.

'There is that, of course. No, Superintendent Battle, I had no motive for wishing Mr Shaitana out of the way. It is really a matter of indifference to me whether he is alive or dead. I thought him a *poseur*, and rather theatrical, and sometimes he irritated me. That is – or rather was – my attitude towards him.'

'That is that, then. Now, Mrs Lorrimer, can you tell me anything about your three companions?'

'I'm afraid not. Major Despard and Miss Meredith I met for the first time tonight. Both of them seem charming people. Dr Roberts I know slightly. He's a very popular doctor, I believe.'

'He is not your own doctor?'

'Oh, no.'

'Now, Mrs Lorrimer, can you tell me how often you got up from your seat tonight, and will you also describe the movements of the other three?'

Mrs Lorrimer did not take any time to think.

'I thought you would probably ask me that. I have been trying to think it out. I got up once myself when I was dummy. I went over to the fire. Mr Shaitana was alive then. I mentioned to him how nice it was to see a wood fire.'

'And he answered?'

'That he hated radiators.'

'Did any one overhear your conversation?'

'I don't think so. I lowered my voice, not to interrupt the players.' She added dryly: 'In fact, you have only my word for it that Mr Shaitana *was* alive and spoke to me.'

Superintendent Battle made no protest. He went on with his quiet methodical questioning.

'What time was that?'

'I should think we had been playing a little over an hour.'

'What about the others?'

'Dr Roberts got me a drink. He also got himself one – that was later. Major Despard also went to get a drink – at about 11.15, I should say.'

'Only once?'

'No – twice, I think. The men moved about a fair amount – but I didn't notice what they did. Miss Meredith left her seat once only, I think. She went round to look at her partner's hand.'

'But she remained near the bridge table?'

'I couldn't say at all. She may have moved away.'

Battle nodded.

'It's all very vague,' he grumbled.

'I am sorry.'

Once again Battle did his conjuring trick and produced the long delicate stiletto.

'Will you look at this, Mrs Lorrimer?'

Mrs Lorrimer took it without emotion.

'Have you ever seen that before?'

'Never.'

'Yet it was lying on a table in the drawing-room.'

'I didn't notice it.'

'You realize, perhaps, Mrs Lorrimer, that with a weapon like that a woman could do the trick just as easily as a man.'

'I suppose she could,' said Mrs Lorrimer quietly.

She leaned forward and handed the dainty little thing back to him.

'But all the same,' said Superintendent Battle, 'the woman would have to be pretty desperate. It was a long chance to take.'

He waited a minute, but Mrs Lorrimer did not speak.

'Do you know anything of the relations between the other three and Mr Shaitana?'

She shook her head.

'Nothing at all.'

'Would you care to give me an opinion as to which of them you consider the most likely person?'

Mrs Lorrimer drew herself up stiffly.

'I should not care to do anything of the kind. I consider that a most improper question.'

The superintendent looked like an abashed little boy who has been reprimanded by his grandmother.

'Address, please,' he mumbled, drawing his notebook towards him.

'111 Cheyne Lane, Chelsea.'

'Telephone number?'

'Chelsea 45632.'

Mrs Lorrimer rose.

'Anything you want to ask, M. Poirot?' said Battle hurriedly.

Mrs Lorrimer paused, her head slightly inclined.

'Would it be a *proper* question, madame, to ask you your opinion of your companions, not as potential murderers but as bridge players?'

Mrs Lorrimer answered coldly:

'I have no objection to answering that – if it bears upon the matter at issue in any way – though I fail to see how it can.'

'I will be the judge of that. Your answer, if you please, madame.'

In the tone of a patient adult humouring an idiot child, Mrs Lorrimer replied:

'Major Despard is a good sound player. Dr Roberts over-calls, but plays his hand brilliantly. Miss Meredith is quite a nice little player, but a bit too cautious. Anything more?'

In his turn doing a conjuring trick, Poirot produced four crumpled bridge scores.

'These scores, madame, is one of these yours?'

She examined them.

'This is my writing. It is the score of the third rubber.'

'And this score?'

'That must be Major Despard's. He cancels as he goes.'

'And this one?'

'Miss Meredith's. The first rubber.'

'So this unfinished one is Dr Roberts'?'

'Yes.'

'Thank you, madame, I think that is all.'

Mrs Lorrimer turned to Mrs Oliver.

'Goodnight, Mrs Oliver. Goodnight, Colonel Race.'

Then, having shaken hands with all four of them, she went out.

CHAPTER SIX

Third Murderer?

'Didn't get any extra change out of her,' commented Battle. 'Put me in my place, too. She's the old-fashioned kind, full of consideration for others, but arrogant as the devil! I can't believe she did it, but you never know! She's got plenty of resolution. What's the idea of the bridge scores, M. Poirot?'

Poirot spread them on the table.

'They are illuminating, do you not think? What do we want in this case? A clue to character. And a clue not to one character, but to four characters. And this is where we are most likely to find it – in these scribbled figures. Here is the first rubber, you see – a tame business, soon over. Small neat figures – careful addition and subtraction – that is Miss Meredith's score. She was playing with Mrs Lorrimer. They had the cards, and they won.

'In this next one it is not so easy to follow the play, since it is kept in the cancellation style. But it tells us perhaps something about Major Despard – a man who likes the whole time to know at a glance where he stands. The figures are small and full of character.

'This next score is Mrs Lorrimer's – she and Dr Roberts against the other two – a Homeric combat – figures mounting up above the line each side. Overcalling on the doctor's part, and they go down; but, since they are both first-class players, they never go down very much. If the doctor's overcalling induces rash bidding on the other side there is the chance seized of doubling. See – these figures here are doubled tricks gone down. A characteristic hand-writing, graceful, very legible, firm.

1st Rubber

WE	THEY
(Mrs LORRIMER v MISS MEREDITH)	(MAJOR DESPARD v DR ROBERTS)

WE	THEY
700	
300	
50	
50	
30	

HONOURS

TRICKS

WE	THEY
120	
120	
1370	

1st RUBBER

Score kept by MISS MEREDITH

2nd Rubber

WE	THEY
(MAJOR DESPARD v MRS LORRIMER)	(DR ROBERTS v MISS MEREDITH)

WE	THEY
(11)	
1060	
~~450~~	
~~410~~	
~~440~~	
~~540~~	
~~440~~	
~~560~~	
~~500~~	
~~50~~	

HONOURS

TRICKS

WE	THEY
~~60~~	~~120~~
~~100~~	
70	30
80	

2nd RUBBER

Score kept by MAJOR DESPARD

WE	THEY
DR ROBERTS v MRS LORRIMER	MAJOR DESPARD v MISS MEREDITH
500	
1500	200
100	100
100	200
300	100
500	100
200	60
200	50
30	50
HONOURS	
TRICKS	
	30
	120
100	
280	
3810	1000

(28)

3rd RUBBER
Score kept by MRS LORRIMER

WE	THEY
DR ROBERTS v MISS MEREDITH	MAJOR DESPARD v MRS LORRIMER
50	
100	
100	
50	
200	100
50	50
50	100
	50
HONOURS	
TRICKS	
30	70

4th RUBBER (Unfinished)
Score kept by DR ROBERTS

'Here is the last score – the unfinished rubber. I collected one score in each person's handwriting, you see. Figures rather flamboyant. Not such high scores as the preceding rubber. That is probably because the doctor was playing with Miss Meredith, and she is a timid player. His calling would make her more so!

'You think, perhaps, that they are foolish, these questions that I ask? But it is not so. I want to get at the characters of these four players, and when it is only about bridge I ask, everyone is ready and willing to speak.'

'I never think your questions foolish, M. Poirot,' said Battle. 'I've seen too much of your work. Everyone's got their own ways of working. I know that. I give my inspectors a free hand always. Everyone's got to find out for themselves what method suits them best. But we'd better not discuss that now. We'll have the girl in.'

Anne Meredith was upset. She stopped in the doorway. Her breath came unevenly.

Superintendent Battle was immediately fatherly. He rose, set a chair for her at a slightly different angle.

'Sit down, Miss Meredith, sit down, Now, don't be alarmed. I know all this seems rather dreadful, but it's not so bad, really.'

'I don't think anything could be worse,' said the girl in a low voice. 'It's so awful – so *awful* – to think that *one* of us – that one of *us* –'

'You let me do the thinking,' said Battle kindly. 'Now, then, Miss Meredith, suppose we have your address first of all.'

'Wendon Cottage, Wallingford.'

'No address in town?'

'No, I'm staying at my club for a day or two.'

'And your club is?'

'Ladies' Naval and Military.'

'Good. Now, then, Miss Meredith, how well did you know Mr Shaitana?'

'I didn't know him well at all. I always thought he was a most frightening man.'

'Why?'

'Oh, well he *was*! That awful smile! And a way he had of bending over you. As though he might bite you.'

'Had you known him long?'

'About nine months. I met him in Switzerland during the winter sports.'

'I should never have thought he went in for winter sports,' said Battle, surprised.

'He only skated. He was a marvellous skater. Lots of figures and tricks.'

'Yes, that sounds more like him. And did you see much of him after that?'

'Well – a fair amount. He asked me to parties and things like that. They were rather fun.'

'But you didn't like him himself?'

'No, I thought he was a shivery kind of man.'

Battle said gently:

'But you'd no special reason for being afraid of him?'

Anne Meredith raised wide limpid eyes to his.

'Special reason? Oh, no.'

'That's all right, then. Now about tonight. Did you leave your seat at all?'

'I don't think so. Oh, yes, I may have done once. I went round to look at the other's hands.'

'But you stayed by the bridge table all the time?'

'Yes.'

'Quite sure, Miss Meredith?'

The girl's cheeks flamed suddenly.

'No – no, I think I walked about.'

'Right. You'll excuse me, Miss Meredith, but try and speak the truth. I know you're nervous, and when one's nervous one's apt to – well, to say the thing the way you want it to be. But that doesn't really pay in the end. You walked about. Did you walk over in the direction of Mr Shaitana?'

The girl was silent for a minute, then she said:

'Honestly – *honestly* – I don't remember.'

'Well, we'll leave it that you may have done. Know anything about the other three?'

The girl shook her head.

'I've never seen any of them before.'

'What do you think of them? Any likely murderers amongst them?'

'I can't believe it. I just can't believe it. It couldn't be Major Despard. And I don't believe it could be the doctor – after all, a doctor could kill any one in much easier ways. A drug – or something like that.'

'Then, if it's anyone, you think it's Mrs Lorrimer.'

'Oh, I *don't*. I'm sure she wouldn't. She's so charming – and so kind to play bridge with. She's so good herself, and yet she doesn't make one feel nervous, or point out one's mistakes.'

'Yet you left her name to the last,' said Battle.

'Only because stabbing seems somehow more like a woman.'

Battle did his conjuring trick. Anne Meredith shrank back.

'Oh, horrible. Must I – take it?'

'I'd rather you did.'

He watched her as she took the stiletto gingerly, her face contracted with repulsion.

'With this tiny thing – with this –'

'Go in like butter,' said Battle with gusto. 'A child could do it.'

'You mean – you mean' – wide, terrified eyes fixed themselves on his face – 'that *I* might have done it? But I didn't. Why should I?'

'That's just the question we'd like to know,' said Battle. 'What's the motive? Why did anyone want to kill Shai-

tana? He was a picturesque person, but he wasn't dangerous, as far as I can make out.'

Was there a slight indrawing of her breath – a sudden
lifting of her breast?

'Not a blackmailer, for instance, or anything of that
sort?' went on Battle. 'And anyway, Miss Meredith, you
don't look the sort of girl who's got a lot of guilty secrets.'

For the first time she smiled, reassured by his geniality.

'No, indeed I haven't. I haven't got any secrets at all.'

'Then don't worry, Miss Meredith. We shall have to
come round and ask you a few more questions, I expect,
but it will be all a matter of routine.'

He got up.

'Now off you go. My constable will get you a taxi; and
don't you lie awake worrying yourself. Take a couple of
aspirins.'

He ushered her out. As he came back Colonel Race said
in a low, amused voice:

'Battle, what a really accomplished liar you are! Your
fatherly air was unsurpassed.'

'No good dallying about with her, Colonel Race. Either
the poor kid is dead scared – in which case it's cruelty, and
I'm not a cruel man; I never have been – or she's a highly
accomplished little actress, and we shouldn't get any
further if we were to keep her here half the night.'

Mrs Oliver gave a sigh and ran her hands freely through
her fringe until it stood upright and gave her a wholly
drunken appearance.

'Do you know,' she said, 'I rather believe now that she
did it! It's lucky it's not in a book. They don't really like
the young and beautiful girl to have done it. All the same,
I rather think she did. What do *you* think, M. Poirot?'

'Me, I have just made a discovery.'

'In the bridge scores again?'

'Yes, Miss Anne Meredith turns her score over, draws
lines and uses the back.'

'And what does that mean?'

'It means she has the habit of poverty or else is of a naturally economical turn of mind.'

'She's expensively dressed,' said Mrs Oliver.

'Send in Major Despard,' said Superintendent Battle.

CHAPTER SEVEN

Fourth Murderer?

Despard entered the room with a quick springing step – a step that reminded Poirot of something or some one.

'I'm sorry to have kept you waiting all this while, Major Despard,' said Battle. 'But I wanted to let the ladies get away as soon as possible.'

'Don't apologize. I understand.'

He sat down and looked inquiringly at the superintendent.

'How well did you know Mr Shaitana?' began the latter.

'I've met him twice,' said Despard crisply.

'Only twice?'

'That's all.'

'On what occasions?'

'About a month ago we were both dining at the same house. Then he asked me to a cocktail party a week later.'

'A cocktail party here?'

'Yes.'

'Where did it take place – this room or the drawing-room?'

'In all the rooms.'

'See this little thing lying about?'

Battle once more produced the stiletto.

Major Despard's lip twisted slightly.

'No,' he said. 'I didn't mark it down on that occasion for future use.'

'There's no need to go ahead of what I say, Major Despard.'

'I beg your pardon. The inference was fairly obvious.'

There was a moment's pause, then Battle resumed his inquiries.

'Had you any motive for disliking Mr Shaitana?'

'Every motive.'

'Eh?' The superintendent sounded startled.

'For disliking him – not for killing him,' said Despard. 'I hadn't the least wish to kill him, but I would thoroughly have enjoyed kicking him. A pity. It's too late now.'

'Why did you want to kick him, Major Despard?'

'Because he was the sort of Dago who needed kicking badly. He used to make the toe of my boot fairly itch.'

'Know anything about him – to his discredit, I mean?'

'He was too well dressed – he wore his hair too long – and he smelt of scent.'

'Yet you accepted his invitation to dinner,' Battle pointed out.

'If I were only to dine in houses where I thoroughly approved of my host I'm afraid I shouldn't dine out very much, Superintendent Battle,' said Despard drily.

'You like society, but you don't approve of it? suggested the other.

'I like it for very short periods. To come back from the wilds to lighted rooms and women in lovely clothes, to dancing and good food and laughter – yes, I enjoy that – for a time. And then the insincerity of it all sickens me, and I want to be off again.'

'It must be a dangerous sort of life that you lead, Major Despard, wandering about in these wild places.'

Despard shrugged his shoulders. He smiled slightly.

'Mr Shaitana didn't lead a dangerous life – but he is dead, and I am alive!'

'He may have led a more dangerous life than you think,' said Battle meaningly.

'What do you mean?'

'The late Mr Shaitana was a bit of a Nosey Parker,' said Battle.

The other leaned forward.

'You mean that he meddled with other people's lives – that he discovered – what?'

'I really meant that perhaps he was the sort of man who meddled – er – well, with women.'

Major Despard leant back in his chair. He laughed, an amused but indifferent laugh.

'I don't think women would take a mountebank like that seriously.'

'What's your theory of who killed him, Major Despard?'

'Well, I know I didn't. Little Miss Meredith didn't. I can't imagine Mrs Lorrimer doing so – she reminds me of one of my more God-fearing aunts. That leaves the medical gentleman.'

'Can you describe your own and other people's movements this evening?'

'I got up twice – once for an ash-tray, and I also poked the fire – and once for a drink –'

'At what times?'

'I couldn't say. First time might have been about half-past ten, the second time eleven, but that's pure guesswork. Mrs Lorrimer went over to the fire once and said something to Shaitana. I didn't actually hear him answer, but, then, I wasn't paying attention. I couldn't swear he didn't. Miss Meredith wandered about the room a bit, but I don't think she went over near the fireplace. Roberts was always jumping up and down – three or four times at least.'

'I'll ask you M. Poirot's question,' said Battle with a smile. 'What did you think of them as bridge players?'

'Miss Meredith's quite a good player. Roberts overcalls his hand disgracefully. He deserves to go down more than he does. Mrs Lorrimer's damned good.'

Battle turned to Poirot.

'Anything else, M. Poirot?'

Poirot shook his head.

Despard gave his address as the Albany, wished them goodnight and left the room.

As he closed the door behind him, Poirot made a slight movement.

'What is it?' demanded Battle.

'Nothing,' said Poirot. 'It just occurred to me that he walked like a tiger – yes, just so – lithe, easy, does the tiger move along.'

'H'm!' said Battle. 'Now, then' – his eyes glanced round at his three companions – '*which of 'em did it?*'

CHAPTER EIGHT

Which of Them?

Battle looked from one face to another. Only one person answered his question. Mrs Oliver, never averse to giving her views, rushed into speech.

'The girl or the doctor,' she said.

Battle looked questioningly at the other two. But both the men were unwilling to make a pronouncement. Race shook his head. Poirot carefully smoothed his crumpled bridge scores.

'One of 'em did it,' said Battle musingly. 'One of 'em's lying like hell. But which? It's not easy – no, it's not easy.'

He was silent for a minute or two, then he said:

'If we're to go by what they *say*, the medico thinks Despard did it, Despard thinks the medico did it, the girl thinks Mrs Lorrimer did it – and Mrs Lorrimer won't say! Nothing very illuminating there.'

'Perhaps not,' said Poirot.

Battle shot him a quick glance.

'You think there is?'

Poirot waved an airy hand.

'A *nuance* – nothing more! Nothing to go upon.'

Battle continued:

'You two gentlemen won't say what you think –'

'No evidence,' said Race curtly.

'Oh, you *men*!' sighed Mrs Oliver, despising such reticence.

'Let's look at the rough possibilities,' said Battle. He considered a minute. 'I put the doctor first, I think. Specious sort of customer. Would know the right spot to shove the dagger in. But there's not much more than that to it. Then take Despard. There's a man with any amount of nerve. A man accustomed to quick decisions and a man who's quite at home doing dangerous things. Mrs Lorrmier? She's got any amount of nerve, too, and she's the sort of woman who might have a secret in her life. She looks as though she's known trouble. On the other hand, I'd say she's what I call a high-principled woman – sort of woman who might be headmistress of a girls' school. It isn't easy to think of her sticking a knife into anyone. In fact, I don't think she did. And lastly, there's little Miss Meredith. We don't know anything about her. She seems an ordinary good-looking, rather shy girl. But one doesn't know, as I say, anything about her.'

'We know that Shaitana believed she had committed murder,' said Poirot.

'The angelic face masking the demon,' mused Mrs Oliver.

'This getting us anywhere, Battle?' asked Colonel Race.

'Unprofitable speculation, you think, sir? Well, there's bound to be speculation in a case like this.'

'Isn't it better to find out something about these people?'

Battle smiled.

'Oh, we shall be hard at work on that. I think you could help us there.'

'Certainly. How?'

'As regards Major Despard. He's been abroad a lot – in South America, in East Africa, in South Africa – you've means of knowing those parts. You could get information about him.'

Race nodded.

'It shall be done. I'll get all available data.'

'Oh,' cried Mrs Oliver. 'I've got a plan. There are four of us – four sleuths, as you might say – and four of *them*! How would it be if we each took one. Backed our fancy! Colonel Race takes Major Despard, Superintendent Battle takes Dr Roberts, I'll take Anne Meredith, and M. Poirot takes Mrs Lorrimer. Each of us to follow our own line!'

Superintendent Battle shook his head decisively.

'Couldn't quite do that, Mrs Oliver. That is official, you see. I'm in charge. I've got to investigate *all* lines. Besides, it's all very well to say back your fancy. Two of us might want to back the same horse! Colonel Race hasn't said he suspects Major Despard. And M. Poirot mayn't be putting his money on Mrs Lorrimer.'

Mrs Oliver sighed.

'It was such a good plan,' she sighed regretfully. 'So *neat*.' Then she cheered up a little. 'But you don't mind me doing a little investigating on my own, do you?'

'No,' said Superintendent Battle slowly. 'I can't say I object to that. In fact, it's out of my power to object. Having been at this party tonight, you're naturally free to do anything your own curiosity or interest suggests. But I'd like to point out to you, Mrs Oliver, that you'd better be a little careful.'

'Discretion itself,' said Mrs Oliver. 'I shan't breathe a word of – of anything –' she ended a little lamely.

'I do not think that was quite Superintendent Battle's meaning,' said Hercule Poirot. 'He meant that you will be dealing with a person who has already, to the best of our belief, killed twice. A person, therefore, who will not hesitate to kill a third time – if he considers it necessary.'

Mrs Oliver looked at him thoughtfully. Then she smiled – an agreeable engaging smile, rather like that of an impudent small child.

'You Have Been Warned,' she quoted. 'Thank you, M. Poirot. I'll watch my step. But I'm not going to be out of this.'

Poirot bowed gracefully.

'Permit me to say – you are the sport, madame.'

'I presume,' said Mrs Oliver, sitting up very straight and speaking in a business-like committee-meeting manner, 'that all information we receive will be pooled – that is that we will not keep any knowledge to ourselves. Our own deductions and impressions, of course, we are entitled to keep up our sleeves.'

Superintendent Battle sighed.

'This isn't a detective story, Mrs Oliver,' he said.

Race said:

'Naturally, all information must be handed over to the police.'

Having said this in his most 'Orderly Room' voice, he added with a slight twinkle in his eye: 'I'm sure you'll play fair, Mrs Oliver – the stained glove, the fingerprint on the tooth-glass, the fragment of burnt paper – you'll turn them over to Battle here.'

'You may laugh,' said Mrs Oliver. 'But a woman's intuition –'

She nodded her head with decision.

Race rose to his feet.

'I'll have Despard looked up for you. It may take a little time. Anything else I can do?'

'I don't think so, thank you, sir. You've no hints? I'd value anything of that kind.'

'H'm. Well – I'd keep a special lookout for shooting or poison or accidents, but I expect you're on to that already.'

'I'd made a note of that – yes, sir.'

'Good man, Battle. You don't need me to teach you your job. Goodnight, Mrs Oliver. Goodnight, M. Poirot.'

And with a final nod to Battle, Colonel Race left the room.

'Who is he?' asked Mrs Oliver.

'Very fine Army record,' said Battle. 'Travelled a lot, too. Not many parts of the world he doesn't know about.'

'Secret Service, I suppose,' said Mrs Oliver. 'You can't tell me so – I know; but he wouldn't have been asked otherwise this evening. The four murderers and the four sleuths – Scotland Yard. Secret Service. Private. Fiction. A clever idea.'

Poirot shook his head.

'You are in error, madame. It was a very *stupid* idea. The tiger was alarmed – and the tiger sprang.'

'The tiger? Why the tiger?'

'By the tiger I mean the murderer,' said Poirot.

Battle said bluntly:

'What's *your* idea of the right line to take, M. Poirot? That's one question. And I'd also like to know what you think of the psychology of these four people. You're rather hot on that.'

Still smoothing his bridge scores, Poirot said:

'You are right – psychology is very important. We know the *kind* of murder that has been committed, the *way* it was committed. If we have a person who from the psychological point of view could not have committed that particular type of murder, then we can dismiss that person from our calculations. We know *something* about these people. We have our own impression of them, we know the line that each has elected to take, and we know something about their minds and their characters from what we have learned about them as card players and from the study of their handwriting and of these scores. But alas! it is not too easy to give a definite pronouncement. This murder required audacity and nerve – a person who was willing to take a risk. Well, we have Dr Roberts – a bluffer – an overcaller of his hand – a man with complete confidence in his own powers to pull off a risky thing. His psychology fits very well with the crime. One might say, then, that that automatically wipes out Miss Meredith. She is timid, frightened of over-calling her hand, careful, economical, prudent and lacking in self-confidence. The last type of person to carry out a bold and risky coup. But a timid person will murder out of fear. A frightened nervous person can be made desperate, can turn like a rat at bay if driven into a corner. If Miss Meredith had committed a crime in the past, and if she believed that Mr Shaitana knew the circumstances of that crime and was about to deliver her up to justice she would

61

be wild with terror – she would stick at nothing to save herself. It would be the same result, though brought about through a different reaction – not cool nerve and daring, but desperate panic. Then take Major Despard – a cool, resourceful man willing to try a long shot if he believed it absolutely necessary. He would weigh the pros and cons and might decide that there was a sporting chance in his favour – and he is the type of man to prefer action to inaction, and a man who would never shrink from taking the dangerous way if he believed there was a reasonable chance of success. Finally, there is Mrs Lorrimer, an elderly woman, but a woman in full possession of her wits and faculties. A cool woman. A woman with a mathematical brain. She has probably the best brain of the four. I confess that if Mrs Lorrimer committed a crime, I should expect it to be a *premeditated* crime. I can see her planning a crime slowly and carefully, making sure that there were no flaws in her scheme. For that reason she seems to me slightly more unlikely than the other three. She is, however, the most dominating personality, and whatever she undertook she would probably carry through without a flaw. She is a thoroughly efficient woman.'

He paused:

'So you see, that does not help us much. No – there is only one way in this crime. We must go back into the past.'

Battle sighed.

'You've said it,' he murmured.

'In the opinion of Mr Shaitana, each of those four people had committed murder. Had he evidence? Or was it a guess? We cannot tell. It is unlikely, I think, that he could have had actual evidence in all four cases –'

'I agree with you there,' said Battle, nodding his head. 'That would be a bit too much of a coincidence.'

'I suggest that it might come about this way – murder or a certain form of murder is mentioned, and Mr Shaitana surprised a look on some one's face. He was very quick –

very sensitive to expression. It amuses him to experiment – to probe gently in the course of apparently aimless conversation – he is alert to notice a wince, a reservation, a desire to turn the conversation. Oh, it is easily done. If you suspect a certain secret, nothing is easier than to confirm your suspicion. Every time a word goes home you notice it – *if you are watching for such a thing.*'

'It's the sort of game that would have amused our late friend,' said Battle, nodding.

'We may assume, then, that such was the procedure in one or more cases. He may have come across a piece of actual evidence in another case and followed it up. I doubt whether, in any of the cases, he had sufficient actual knowledge with which, for instance, to have gone to the police.'

'Or it mayn't have been the kind of case,' said Battle. 'Often enough there's a fishy business – we suspect foul play, but we can't ever prove it. Anyway, the course is clear. We've got to go through the records of all these people – and note any deaths that may be significant. I expect you noticed, just as the Colonel did, what Shaitana said at dinner.'

'The black angel,' murmured Mrs Oliver.

'A neat little reference to poison, to accident, to a doctor's opportunities, to shooting accidents. I shouldn't be surprised if he signed his death-warrant when he said those words.'

'It was a nasty sort of pause,' said Mrs Oliver.

'Yes,' said Poirot. 'Those words went home to one person at least – that person probably thought that Shaitana knew far more than he really did. That listener thought that they were the prelude to the end – that the party was a dramatic entertainment arranged by Shaitana leading up to arrest for murder as its climax! Yes, as you say, he signed his death-warrant when he baited his guests with those words.'

There was a moment's silence.

'This will be a long business,' said Battle with a sigh. 'We can't find out all we want in a moment – and we've got to be careful. We don't want any of the four to suspect what we're doing. All our questioning and so on must seem to have to do with *this* murder. There mustn't be a suspicion that we've got any idea of the motive for the crime. And the devil of it is we've got to check up on four possible murders in the past, not one.'

Poirot demurred.

'Our friend Mr Shaitana was not infallible,' he said. 'He may – it is just possible – have made a mistake.'

'About all four?'

'No – he was more intelligent than that.'

'Call it fifty-fifty?'

'Not even that. For me, I say one in four.'

'One innocent and three guilty? That's bad enough. And the devil of it is, even if we get at the truth it mayn't help us. Even if somebody did push their great-aunts down the stairs in 1912, it won't be much use to us in 1937.'

'Yes, yes, it will be of use to us.' Poirot encouraged him. 'You know that. You know it as well as I do.'

Battle nodded slowly.

'I know what you mean,' he said. 'Same hall-mark.'

'Do you mean,' said Mrs Oliver, 'that the former victim will have been stabbed with a dagger too?'

'Not quite as crude as that, Mrs Oliver,' said Battle turning to her. 'But I don't doubt it will be essentially the same *type* of crime. The *details* may be different, but the essentials underlying them will be the same. It's odd, but a criminal gives himself away every time by that.'

'Man is an unoriginal animal,' said Hercule Poirot.

'Women,' said Mrs Oliver, 'are capable of infinite variation. I should never commit the same type of murder twice running.'

'Don't you ever write the same plot twice running?' asked Battle.

'*The Lotus Murder*,' murmured Poirot. '*The Clue of the Candle Wax.*'

Mrs Oliver turned on him, her eyes beaming appreciation.

'That's clever of you – that's really very clever of you. Because, of course, those two are exactly the same plot – but nobody else has seen it. One is stolen papers at an informal weekend party of the Cabinet, and the other's a murder in Borneo in a rubber planter's bungalow.'

'But the essential point on which the story turns is the same,' said Poirot. 'One of your neatest tricks. The rubber planter arranges his own murder – the Cabinet Minister arranges the robbery of his own papers. At the last minute the third person steps in and turns deception into reality.'

'I enjoyed your last, Mrs Oliver,' said Superintendent Battle kindly. 'The one where all the Chief Constables were shot simultaneously. You just slipped up once or twice on official details. I know you're keen on accuracy, so I wondered if –'

Mrs Oliver interrupted him.

'As a matter of fact I don't care two pins about accuracy. Who is accurate? Nobody nowadays. If a reporter writes that a beautiful girl of twenty-two dies by turning on the gas after looking out over the sea and kissing her favourite labrador, Bob, goodbye, does anybody make a fuss because the girl was twenty-six, the room faced inland, and the dog was a Sealyham terrier called Bonnie? If a journalist can do that sort of thing, I don't see that it matters if I mix up police ranks and say a revolver when I mean an automatic, and a dictograph when I mean a phonograph, and use a poison that just allows you to gasp one dying sentence and no more. What really matters is plenty of *bodies*! If the thing's getting a little dull, some more blood cheers it up. Somebody is going to tell something – and then they're killed first. That always goes down well. It comes in all my books – camouflaged different ways, of course. And people *like* untraceable poisons, and idiotic police inspectors and girls tied up in cellars with sewer gas or water pouring in (such a troublesome way of killing any one really) and a hero who can dispose of anything from three to seven villains single-handed. I've written thirty-two books by now – and of course they're all exactly the same really, as M. Poirot seems to have noticed – but nobody else has – and I only regret one thing – making my detective a Finn. I don't really know anything about Finns and I'm always getting letters from Finland pointing out something impossible that he's said or done. They seem to read detective stories a good deal in Finland. I suppose it's the long winters with no daylight. In Bulgaria and Romania they don't seem to read at all. I'd have done better to have made him a Bulgar.'

She broke off.

'I'm so sorry. I'm talking shop. And this is a real murder.' Her face lit up. 'What a good idea it would be if none of them had murdered him. If he'd asked them all, and then quietly committed suicide just for the fun of making a schemozzle.'

Poirot nodded approvingly.

'An admirable solution. So neat. So ironic. But, alas, Mr Shaitana was not that sort of man. He was very fond of life.'

'I don't think he was really a nice man,' said Mrs Oliver slowly.

'He was not nice, no,' said Poirot. 'But he was alive – and now he is dead, and as I told him once, I have a *bourgeois* attitude to murder, I disapprove of it.'

He added softly:

'And so – I am prepared to go inside the tiger's cage . . .'

CHAPTER NINE

Dr Roberts

'Good morning, Superintendent Battle.'

Dr Roberts rose from his chair and offered a large pink hand smelling of a mixture of good soap and faint carbolic.

'How are things going?' he went on.

Superintendent Battle glanced round the comfortable consulting-room before answering.

'Well, Dr Roberts, strictly speaking, they're not going. They're standing still.'

'There's been nothing much in the papers, I've been glad to see.'

'*Sudden death of the well-known Mr Shaitana at an evening party in his own home*. It's left at that for the moment. We've had the autopsy – I brought a report of the findings along – thought it might interest you –'

'That's very kind of you – it would – h'm – h'm. Yes, very interesting.'

He handed it back.

'And we've interviewed Mr Shaitana's solicitor. We know the terms of his will. Nothing of interest there. He has relatives in Syria, it seems. And then, of course, we've been through all his private papers.'

Was it fancy or did that broad, clean-shaven countenance look a little strained – a little wooden?

'And?' said Dr Roberts.

'Nothing,' said Superintendent Battle, watching him. There wasn't a sigh of relief. Nothing so blatant as that. But the doctor's figure seemed to relax just a shade more comfortably in his chair.

'And so you've come to me?'

'And so, as you say, I've come to you.'

The doctor's eyebrows rose a little and his shrewd eyes looked into Battle's.

'Want to go through *my* private papers – eh?'

'That was my idea.'

'Got a search warrant?'

'No.'

'Well; you could get one easily enough, I suppose. I'm not going to make difficulties. It's not very pleasant being suspected of murder but I suppose I can't blame you for what's obviously your duty.'

'Thank you, sir,' said Superintendent Battle with real gratitude. 'I appreciate your attitude, if I may say so, very much. I hope all the others will be as reasonable, I'm sure.'

'What can't be cured must be endured,' said the doctor good-humouredly.

He went on:

'I've finished seeing my patients here. I'm just off on my rounds. I'll leave you my keys and just say a word to my secretary and you can rootle to your heart's content.'

'That's all very nice and pleasant, I'm sure,' said Battle. 'I'd like to ask you a few more questions before you go.'

'About the other night? Really, I told you all I know.'

'No, not about the other night. About yourself.'

'Well, man, ask away, what do you want to know?'

'I'd just like a rough sketch of your career, Dr Roberts. Birth, marriage, and so on.'

'It will get me into practice for *Who's Who*,' said the doctor dryly. 'My career's a perfectly straightforward one. I'm a Shropshire man, born at Ludlow. My father was in practice there. He died when I was fifteen. I was educated at Shrewsbury and went in for medicine like my father before me. I'm a St Christopher's man – but you'll have all the medical details already, I expect.'

'I looked you up, yes, sir. You an only child or have you any brothers or sisters?'

'I'm an only child. Both my parents are dead and I'm unmarried. Will that do to get on with? I came into partnership here with Dr Emery. He retired about fifteen years ago. Lives in Ireland. I'll give you his address if you like. I live here with a cook, a parlourmaid and a housemaid. My secretary comes in daily. I make a good income and I only kill a reasonable number of my patients. How's that?'

Superintendent Battle grinned.

'That's fairly comprehensive, Dr Roberts. I'm glad you've got a sense of humour. Now I'm going to ask you one more thing.'

'I'm a strictly moral man, superintendent.'

'Oh, that wasn't my meaning. No, I was going to ask you if you'd give me the names of four friends – people who've known you intimately for a number of years. Kind of references, if you know what I mean.'

'Yes, I think so. Let me see now. You'd prefer people who are actually in London now?'

'It would make it a bit easier, but it doesn't really matter.'

The doctor thought for a minute or two, then with his fountain pen he scribbled four names and addresses on a sheet of paper and pushed it across the desk to Battle.

'Will those do? They're the best I can think of on the spur of the moment.'

Battle read carefully, nodded his head in satisfaction and put the sheet of paper away in an inner pocket.

'It's just a question of elimination,' he said. 'The sooner I can get one person eliminated and go on to the next, the better it is for every one concerned. I've got to make perfectly certain that you weren't on bad terms with the late Mr Shaitana, that you had no private connections or business dealings with him, that there was no question of his having injured you at any time and your bearing resentment. *I* may believe you when you say you only knew him slightly – but it isn't a question of *my* belief. I've got to say I've made *sure*.'

'Oh, I understand perfectly. You've got to think everybody's a liar till he's proved he's speaking the truth. Here are my keys, superintendent. That's the drawers of the desk – that's the bureau – that little one's the key of the poison cupboard. Be sure to lock it up again. Perhaps I'd better just have a word with my secretary.'

He pressed a button on his desk.

Almost immediately the door opened and a competent-looking young woman appeared.

'You rang, doctor?'

'This is Miss Burgess – Superintendent Battle from Scotland Yard.'

Miss Burgess turned a cool gaze on Battle. It seemed to say:

'Dear me, what sort of an animal is this?'

'I should be glad, Miss Burgess, if you will answer any questions Superintendent Battle may put to you, and give him any help he may need.'

'Certainly, if you say so, doctor.'

'Well,' said Roberts, rising, 'I'll be off. Did you put the morphia in my case? I shall need it for the Lockheart case.'

He bustled out, still talking, and Miss Burgess followed him.

'Will you press that button when you want me, Superintendent Battle?'

Superintendent Battle thanked her and said he would do so. Then he set to work.

His search was careful and methodical, though he had no great hopes of finding anything of importance. Roberts' ready acquiescence dispelled the chance of that. Roberts was no fool. He would realize that a search would be bound to come and he would make provisions accordingly. There was, however, a faint chance that Battle might come across a hint of the information he was really after, since Roberts would not know the real object of his search.

Superintendent Battle opened and shut drawers, rifled pigeon-holes, glanced through a chequebook, estimated the unpaid bills – noted what those same bills were for, scrutinized Roberts' passbook, ran through his case notes and generally left no written document unturned. The result was meagre in the extreme. He next took a look through the poison cupboard, noted the wholesale firms with which the doctor dealt, and the system of checking, relocked the cupboard and passed on to the bureau. The contents of the latter were of a more personal nature, but Battle found nothing germane to his search. He shook his head, sat down in the doctor's chair and pressed the desk button.

Miss Burgess appeared with commendable promptitude.

Superintendent Battle asked her politely to be seated and then sat studying her for a moment, before he decided which way to tackle her. He had sensed immediately her hostility and he was uncertain whether to provoke her into unguarded speech by increasing that hostility or whether to try a softer method of approach.

'I suppose you know what all this is about, Miss Burgess?' he said at last.

'Dr Roberts told me,' said Miss Burgess shortly.

'The whole thing's rather delicate,' said Superintendent Battle.

'Is it?' said Miss Burgess.

'Well, it's rather a nasty business. Four people are under suspicion and one of them must have done it. What I want to know is whether you've ever seen this Mr Shaitana?'

'Never.'

'Ever heard Dr Roberts speak of him?'

'Never – no, I am wrong. About a week ago Dr Roberts told me to enter up a dinner appointment in his engagement-book. Mr Shaitana, 8.15, on the 18th.'

'And that is the first you ever heard of this Mr Shaitana?'

'Yes.'

'Never seen his name in the papers? He was often in the fashionable news.'

'I've got better things to do than reading the fashionable news.'

'I expect you have. Oh, I expect you have,' said the superintendent mildly.

'Well,' he went on. 'There it is. All four of these people will only admit to knowing Mr Shaitana slightly. But one of them knew him well enough to kill him. It's my job to find out which of them it was.'

There was an unhelpful pause. Miss Burgess seemed quite uninterested in the performance of Superintendent Battle's job. It was her job to obey her employer's orders and sit here listening to what Superintendent Battle chose to say and answer any direct questions he might choose to put to her.

'You know, Miss Burgess,' the superintendent found it uphill work but he persevered, 'I doubt if you appreciate half the difficulties of our job. People say things, for instance. Well, we mayn't believe a word of it, but we've got to take notice of it all the same. It's particularly noticeable in a case of this kind. I don't want to say anything against your sex but there's no doubt that a woman, when she's rattled, is apt to lash out with her tongue a bit. She makes unfounded accusations, hints this, that and the other, and rakes up all sorts of old scandals that have probably nothing whatever to do with the case.'

'Do you mean,' demanded Miss Burgess, 'that one of these other people has been saying things against the doctor?'

'Not exactly *said* anything,' said Battle cautiously. 'But all the same, I'm bound to take notice. Suspicious circumstances about the death of a patient. Probably all a lot of nonsense. I'm ashamed to bother the doctor with it.'

'I suppose some one's got hold of that story about Mrs Graves,' said Miss Burgess wrathfully. 'The way people talk about things they know nothing whatever about is disgraceful. Lots of old ladies get like that – they think everybody is poisoning them – their relations and their servants and even their doctors. Mrs Graves had had three doctors before she came to Dr Roberts and then when she got the same fancies about him he was quite willing for her to have Dr Lee instead. It's the only thing to do in these cases, he said. And after Dr Lee she had Dr Steele, and then Dr Farmer – until she died, poor old thing.'

'You'd be surprised the way the smallest thing starts a story,' said Battle. 'Whenever a doctor benefits by the death of a patient somebody has something ill-natured to say. And yet why shouldn't a grateful patient leave a little something, or even a big something to her medical attendant.'

'It's the relations,' said Miss Burgess. 'I always think there's nothing like death for bringing out the meanness of human nature. Squabbling over who's to have what before the body's cold. Luckily, Dr Roberts has never had any trouble of that kind. He always says he hopes his patients won't leave him anything. I believe he once had a legacy of fifty pounds and he's had two walking sticks and a gold watch, but nothing else.'

'It's a difficult life, that of a professional man,' said Battle with a sigh. 'He's always open to blackmail. The most innocent occurrences lend themselves sometimes to a scandalous appearance. A doctor's got to avoid even the appearance of evil – that means he's got to have his wits about him good and sharp.'

'A lot of what you say is true,' said Miss Burgess. 'Doctors have a difficult time with hysterical women.'

'Hysterical women. That's right. I thought in my own mind, that that was all it amounted to.'

'I suppose you mean that dreadful Mrs Craddock?'

Battle pretended to think.

'Let me see, was it three years ago? No, more.'

'Four or five, I think. She was a *most* unbalanced woman! I was glad when she went abroad and so was Dr Roberts. She told her husband the most frightful lies – they always

73

do, of course. Poor man, he wasn't quite himself – he'd begun to be ill. He died of anthrax, you know, an infected shaving brush.'

'I'd forgotten that,' said Battle untruthfully.

'And then she went abroad and died not long afterwards. But I always thought she was a nasty type of woman – man-mad, you know.'

'I know the kind,' said Battle. 'Very dangerous, they are. A doctor's got to give them a wide berth. Whereabouts did she die abroad – I seem to remember.'

'Egypt, I think it was. She got blood-poisoning – some native infection.'

'Another thing that must be difficult for a doctor,' said Battle, making a conversational leap, 'is when he suspects that one of his patients is being poisoned by one of their relatives. What's he to do? He's got to be sure – or else hold his tongue. And if he's done the latter, then it's awkward for him if there's talk of foul play afterwards. I wonder if any case of that kind has ever come Dr Roberts' way?'

'I really don't think it has,' said Miss Burgess, considering. 'I've never heard of anything like that.'

'From the statistical point of view, it would be interesting to know how many deaths occur among a doctor's practice per year. For instance now, you've been with Dr Roberts some years –'

'Seven.'

'Seven. Well, how many deaths have there been in that time off-hand?'

'Really, it's difficult to say.' Miss Burgess gave herself up to calculation. She was by now quite thawed and un-suspicious. 'Seven, eight – of course, I can't remember exactly – I shouldn't say more than thirty in the time.'

'Then I fancy Dr Roberts must be a better doctor than most,' said Battle genially. 'I suppose, too, most of his patients are upper-class. They can afford to take care of themselves.'

'He's a very popular doctor. He's so good at diagnosis.'

Battle sighed and rose to his feet.

'I'm afraid I've been wandering from my duty, which is to find out a connection between the doctor and this Mr Shaitana. You're quite sure he wasn't a patient of the doctor's?'

'Quite sure.'

'Under another name, perhaps?' Battle handed her a photograph. 'Recognize him at all?'

'What a very theatrical-looking person. No, I've never seen him here at any time.'

'Well, that's that.' Battle sighed. 'I'm much obliged to the doctor, I'm sure, for being so pleasant about everything. Tell him from me, will you? Tell him I'm passing on to No. 2. Goodbye, Miss Burgess, and thank you for your help.'

He shook hands and departed. Walking along the street he took a small notebook from his pocket and made a couple of entries in it under the letter R.

Mrs Graves? Unlikely.
Mrs Craddock?
No legacies.
No wife. (Pity.)
Investigate deaths of patients. Difficult.

He closed the book and turned into the Lancaster Gate branch of the London and Wessex Bank.

The display of his official card brought him to a private interview with the manager.

'Good morning, sir. One of your clients is a Dr Geoffrey Roberts, I understand.'

'Quite correct, superintendent.'

'I shall want some information about that gentleman's account going back over a period of years.'

'I will see what I can do for you.'

A complicated half-hour followed. Finally Battle, with a sigh, tucked away a sheet of pencilled figures.

'Got what you want?' inquired the bank manager curiously.

'No, I haven't. Not one suggestive lead. Thank you all the same.'

At that same moment, Dr Roberts, washing his hands in his consulting-room, said over his shoulder to Miss Burgess:

'What about our stolid sleuth, eh? Did he turn the place upside down and you inside out?'

'He didn't get much out of me, I can tell you,' said Miss Burgess, setting her lips tightly.

'My dear girl, no need to be an oyster. I told you to tell him all he wanted to know. What did he want to know, by the way?'

'Oh, he kept harping on your knowing that man Shaitana – suggested even that he might have come here as a patient under a different name. He showed me his photograph. Such a theatrical-looking man!'

'Shaitana? Oh, yes, fond of posing as a modern Mephistopheles. It went down rather well on the whole. What else did Battle ask you?'

'Really nothing very much. Except – oh, yes, somebody had been telling him some absurd nonsense about Mrs Graves – you know the way she used to go on.'

'Graves? Graves? Oh, yes, old Mrs Graves. That's rather funny!' The doctor laughed with considerable amusement. 'That's really very funny indeed.'

And in high good humour he went in to lunch.

CHAPTER TEN

Dr Roberts (continued)

Superintendent Battle was lunching with M. Hercule Poirot.

The former looked downcast, the latter sympathetic.

'Your morning, then, has not been entirely successful,' said Poirot thoughtfully.

Battle shook his head.

'It's going to be uphill work, M. Poirot.'

'What do you think of him?'

'Of the doctor? Well, frankly, I think Shaitana was right. He's a killer. Reminds me of Westaway. And of that lawyer chap in Norfolk. Same hearty, self-confident manner. Same popularity. Both of them were clever devils – so's Roberts. All the same, it doesn't follow that Roberts killed Shaitana – and as a matter of fact I don't think he did. He'd know the risk too well – better than a layman would – that Shaitana might wake and cry out. No, I don't think Roberts murdered him.'

'But you think he has murdered some one?'

'Possibly quite a lot of people. Westaway had. But it's going to be hard to get at. I've looked over his bank account – nothing suspicious there – no large sums suddenly paid in. At any rate, in the last seven years he's not had any legacy from a patient. That wipes out murder for direct gain. He's never married – that's a pity – so ideally simple for a doctor to kill his own wife. He's well-to-do, but then he's got a thriving practice among well-to-do people.'

'In fact he appears to lead a thoroughly blameless life – and perhaps does do so.'

'Maybe. But I prefer to believe the worst.'

He went on:

'There's the hint of a scandal over a woman – one of his patients – name of Craddock. That's worth looking up, I think. I'll get some one on to that straightaway. Woman actually died out in Egypt of some local disease so I don't think there's anything in that – but it might throw a light on his general character and morals.'

'Was there a husband?'

'Yes. Husband died of anthrax.'

'Anthrax?'

'Yes, there were a lot of cheap shaving brushes on the market just then – some of them infected. There was a regular scandal about it.'

'Convenient,' suggested Poirot.

'That's what I thought. If her husband were threatening to kick up a row – But there, it's all conjecture. We haven't a leg to stand upon.'

'Courage, my friend. I know your patience. In the end, you will have perhaps as many legs as a centipede.'

'And fall into the ditch as a result of thinking about them,' grinned Battle.

Then he asked curiously:

'What about you, M. Poirot? Going to take a hand?'

'I, too, might call on Dr Roberts.'

'Two of us in one day. That ought to put the wind up him.'

'Oh, I shall be very discreet. I shall not inquire into his past life.'

'I'd like to know just exactly what line you'll take,' said Battle curiously, 'but don't tell me unless you want to.'

'*Du tout – du tout*. I am most willing. I shall talk a little of bridge, that is all.'

'Bridge again. You harp on that, don't you, M. Poirot?'

'I find the subject very useful.'

'Well, every man to his taste. I don't deal much in the fancy approaches. They don't suit my style.'

'What is your style, superintendent?'

The superintendent met the twinkle in Poirot's eyes with an answering twinkle in his own.

'A straightforward, honest, zealous officer doing his duty in the most laborious manner – that's my style. No frills. No fancy work. Just honest perspiration. Stolid and a bit stupid – that's my ticket.'

Poirot raised his glass.

'To our respective methods – and may success crown our joint efforts.'

'I expect Colonel Race may get us something worth having about Despard,' said Battle. 'He's got a good many sources of information.'

'And Mrs Oliver?'

'Bit of a toss-up there. I rather like that woman. Talks a lot of nonsense, but she's a sport. And women get to know things about other women that men can't get at. She may spot something useful.'

They separated. Battle went back to Scotland Yard to issue instructions for certain lines to be followed up. Poirot betook himself to 200 Gloucester Terrace.

Dr Roberts' eyebrows rose comically as he greeted his guest.

'Two sleuths in one day,' he asked. 'Handcuffs by this evening, I suppose.'

Poirot smiled.

'I can assure you, Dr Roberts, that my attentions are being equally divided between all four of you.'

'That's something to be thankful for, at all events. Smoke?'

'If you permit, I prefer my own.'

Poirot lighted one of his tiny Russian cigarettes.

'Well, what can I do for you?' asked Roberts.

Poirot was silent for a minute or two puffing, then he said:

'Are you a keen observer of human nature, doctor?'

'I don't know. I suppose I am. A doctor has to be.'

'That was exactly my reasoning. I said to myself, "A doctor has always to be studying his patients – their expressions, their colour, how fast they breathe, any signs of restlessness – a doctor notices these things automatically almost without noticing he notices! Dr Roberts is the man to help me.'

'I'm willing enough to help. What's the trouble?'

Poirot produced from a neat little pocket-case three carefully folded bridge scores.

'These are the first three rubbers the other evening,' he explained. 'Here is the first one – in Miss Meredith's handwriting. Now can you tell me – with this to refresh your memory – exactly what the calling was and how each hand went?'

Roberts stared at him in astonishment.

'You're joking, M. Poirot. How can I possibly remember?'

'Can't you? I should be very grateful if you could. Take this first rubber. The first game must have resulted in a game call in hearts or spades, or else one or other side must have gone down fifty.'

'Let me see – that was the first hand. Yes, I think they went out in spades.'

'And the next hand?'

'I suppose one or other of us went down fifty – but I can't remember which or what it was in. Really, M. Poirot, you can hardly expect me to do so.'

'Can't you remember any of the calling or the hands?'

'I got a grand slam – I remember that. It was doubled too. And I also remember going down a nasty smack – playing three no trumps, I think it was – went down a packet. But that was later on.'

'Do you remember with whom you were playing?'

'Mrs Lorrimer. She looked a bit grim, I remember. Didn't like my overcalling, I expect.'

80

'And you can't remember any other of the hands or the calling?'

Roberts laughed.

'My dear M. Poirot, did you really expect I could. First there was the murder – enough to drive the most spectacular hands out of one's mind – and in addition I've played at least half a dozen rubbers since then.'

Poirot sat looking rather crestfallen.

'I'm sorry,' said Roberts.

'It does not matter very much,' said Poirot slowly. 'I hoped that you might remember one or two, at least, of the hands, because I thought they might be valuable landmarks in remembering other things.'

'What other things?'

'Well you might have noticed, for instance, that your partner made a mess of playing a perfectly simple no trumper, or that an opponent, say, presented you with a couple of unexpected tricks by failing to lead an obvious card.'

Dr Roberts became suddenly serious. He leaned forward in his chair.

'Ah,' he said. 'Now I see what you're driving at. Forgive me. I thought at first you were talking pure nonsense. You mean that the murder – the successful accomplishment of the murder – might have made a definite difference in the guilty party's play?'

Poirot nodded.

'You have seized the idea correctly. It would be a clue of the first excellence if you had been four players who knew each other's game well. A variation, a sudden lack of brilliance, a missed opportunity – that would have been immediately noticed. Unluckily, you were all strangers to each other. Variation in play would not be so noticeable. But think, M. le docteur, I beg of you to *think*. Do you remember any inequalities – any sudden glaring mistakes – in the play of anyone?'

There was silence for a minute or two, then Dr Roberts shook his head.

'It's no good. I can't help you,' he said frankly. 'I simply don't remember. All I can tell you is what I told you before: Mrs Lorrimer is a first-class player – she never made a slip that I noticed. She was brilliant from start to finish. Despard's play was uniformly good too. Rather a conventional player – that is, his bidding is strictly conventional. He never steps outside the rules. Won't take a long chance. Miss Meredith –' He hesitated.

'Yes? Miss Meredith?' Poirot prompted him.

'She did make mistakes – once or twice – I remember – towards the end of the evening, but that may simply have been because she was tired – not being a very experienced player. Her hand shook, too –'

He stopped.

'When did her hand shake?'

'When was it now? I can't remember . . . I think she was just nervous. M. Poirot, you're making me imagine things.'

'I apologize. There is another point on which I seek your help.'

'Yes?'

Poirot said slowly:

'It is difficult. I do not, you see, wish to ask you a leading question. If I say, did you notice so and so – well, I have put the thing into your head. Your answer will not be so valuable. Let me try to get at the matter another way. If you will be so kind, Dr Roberts, describe to me the contents of the room in which you played.'

Roberts looked thoroughly astonished.

'The contents of the room?'

'If you will be so good.'

'My dear fellow, I simply don't know where to begin.'

'Begin anywhere you choose.'

'Well, there was a good deal of furniture –'

'*Non, non, non*, be precise, I pray of you.'

Dr Roberts sighed.

He began facetiously after the manner of an auctioneer.

'One large settee upholstered in ivory brocade – one ditto in green ditto – four or five large chairs. Eight or nine Persian rugs – a set of twelve small gilt Empire chairs. William and Mary bureau. (I feel just like an auctioneer's clerk.) Very beautiful Chinese cabinet. Grand piano. There was other furniture but I'm afraid I didn't notice it. Six first-class Japanese prints. Two Chinese pictures on looking-glass. Five or six very beautiful snuff-boxes. Some Japanese ivory netsuke figures on a table by themselves. Some old silver – Charles I. tazzas, I think. One or two pieces of Battersea enamel –'

'Bravo, bravo!' Poirot applauded.

'A couple of old English slipware birds – and, I think, a Ralph Wood figure. Then there was some Eastern stuff – intricate silver work. Some jewellery, I don't know much about that. Some Chelsea birds, I remember. Oh, and some miniatures in a case – pretty good ones, I fancy. That's not all by a long way – but it's all I can think of for the minute.'

'It is magnificent,' said Poirot with due appreciation. 'You have the true observer's eye.'

The doctor asked curiously:

'Have I included the object you had in mind?'

'That is the interesting thing about it,' said Poirot. 'If you had mentioned the object I had in mind it would have been extremely surprising to me. As I thought, you could not mention it.'

'Why?'

Poirot twinkled.

'Perhaps – because it was not there to mention.'

Roberts stared.

'That seems to remind me of something.'

'It reminds you of Sherlock Holmes, does it not? The curious incident of the dog in the night. The dog did not howl in the night. That is the curious thing! Ah, well, I am not above stealing the tricks of others.'

'Do you know, M. Poirot, I am completely at sea as to what you are driving at.'

'That is excellent, that. In confidence, that is how I get my little effects.'

Then, as Dr Roberts still looked rather dazed, Poirot said with a smile as he rose to his feet:

'You may at least comprehend this, what you have told me is going to be very helpful to me in my next interview.'

The doctor rose also.

'I can't see how, but I'll take your word for it,' he said.

They shook hands.

Poirot went down the steps of the doctor's house, and hailed a passing taxi.

'111 Cheyne Lane, Chelsea,' he told the driver.

CHAPTER ELEVEN

Mrs Lorrimer

111 Cheyne Lane was a small house of very neat and trim appearance standing in a quiet street. The door was painted black and the steps were particularly well whitened, the brass of the knocker and handle gleamed in the afternoon sun.

The door was opened by an elderly parlourmaid with an immaculate white cap and apron.

In answer to Poirot's inquiry she said that her mistress was at home.

She preceded him up the narrow staircase.

'What name, sir?'

'M. Hercule Poirot.'

He was ushered into a drawing-room of the usual L shape. Poirot looked about him, noting details. Good furniture, well polished, of the old family type. Shiny chintz on the chairs and settees. A few silver photograph frames about in the old-fashioned manner. Otherwise an agreeable amount of space and light, and some really beautiful chrysanthemums arranged in a tall jar.

Mrs Lorrimer came forward to meet him.

She shook hands without showing any particular surprise at seeing him, indicated a chair, took one herself and remarked favourably on the weather.

There was a pause.

'I hope, madame,' said Hercule Poirot, 'that you will forgive this visit.'

Looking directly at him, Mrs Lorrimer asked:

'Is this a professional visit?'

'I confess it.'

'You realize, I suppose, M. Poirot, that though I shall

85

naturally give Superintendent Battle and the official police any information and help they may require, I am by no means bound to do the same for any unofficial investigator?'

'I am quite aware of that fact, madame. If you show me the door, me, I march to that door with complete submission.'

Mrs Lorrimer smiled very slightly.

'I am not yet prepared to go to those extremes, M. Poirot. I can give you ten minutes. At the end of that time I have to go out to a bridge party.'

'Ten minutes will be ample for my purpose. I want you to describe to me, madame, the room in which you played bridge the other evening – the room in which Mr Shaitana was killed.'

Mrs Lorrimer's eyebrows rose.

'What an extraordinary question! I do not see the point of it.'

'Madame, if when you were playing bridge, some one were to say to you – why do you play that ace or why do you put on the knave that is taken by the queen and not the king which would take the trick? If people were to ask you such questions, the answers would be rather long and tedious, would they not?'

Mrs Lorrimer smiled slightly.

'Meaning that in this game you are the expert and I am the novice. Very well.' She reflected a minute. 'It was a large room. There were a good many things in it.'

'Can you describe some of those things?'

'There were some glass flowers – modern – rather beautiful . . . And I think there were some Chinese or Japanese pictures. And there was a bowl of tiny red tulips – amazingly early for them.'

'Anything else?'

'I'm afraid I didn't notice anything in detail.'

'The furniture – do you remember the colour of the upholstery?'

'Something silky, I think. That's all I can say.'

'Did you notice any of the small objects?'

'I'm afraid not. There were so many. I know it struck me as quite a collector's room.'

There was silence for a minute. Mrs Lorrimer said with a faint smile:

'I'm afraid I have not been very helpful.'

'There is something else.' He produced the bridge scores. 'Here are the first three rubbers played. I wondered if you could help me with the aid of these scores to reconstruct the hands.'

'Let me see.' Mrs Lorrimer looked interested. She bent over the scores.

'That was the first rubber. Miss Meredith and I were playing against the two men. The first game was played in four spades. We made it and an over trick. Then the next hand was left at two diamonds and Dr Roberts went down one trick on it. There was quite a lot of bidding on the third hand, I remember. Miss Meredith passed. Major Despard went a heart. I passed. Dr Roberts gave a jump bid of three clubs. Miss Meredith went three spades. Major Despard bid four diamonds. I doubled. Dr Roberts took it into four hearts. They went down one.'

'*Epatant*,' said Poirot. 'What a memory!'

Mrs Lorrimer went on, disregarding him:

'On the next hand Major Despard passed and I bid a no trump. Dr Roberts bid three hearts. My partner said nothing. Despard put his partner to four. I doubled and they went down two tricks. Then I dealt and we went out on a four-spade call.'

She took up the next score.

'It is difficult, that,' said Poirot. 'Major Despard scores in the cancellation manner.'

'I rather fancy both sides went down fifty to start with – then Dr Roberts went to five diamonds and we doubled and got him down to three tricks. Then we made three clubs, but immediately after the others went game in spades. We made the second game in five clubs. Then we went down a hundred. The others made one heart, we made two no trumps and we finally won the rubber with a four-club call.'

She picked up the next score.

'This rubber was rather a battle, I remember. It started tamely. Major Despard and Miss Meredith made a one-heart call. Then we went down a couple of fifties trying for four hearts and four spades. Then the others made game in spades – no use trying to stop them. We went down three hands running after that but undoubled. Then we won the second game in no trumps. Then a battle royal started. Each side went down in turn. Dr Roberts overcalled but though he went down badly once or twice, his calling paid, for more than once he frightened Miss Meredith out of bidding her hand. Then he bid an original two spades, I gave him three diamonds, he bid four no trumps, I bid five spades and he suddenly jumped to seven diamonds. We were doubled, of course. He had no business to make such a call. By a kind of miracle we got it. I never thought we should when I saw his hand go down. If the others had led a heart we would have been three tricks down. As it was they led the king of clubs and we got it. It was really very exciting.'

'*Je crois bien* – a Grand Slam Vulnerable doubled. It causes the emotions, that! Me, I admit it, I have not the nerve to go for the slams. I content myself with the game.'

'Oh, but you shouldn't,' said Mrs Lorrimer with energy. 'You must play the game properly.'

'Take risks, you mean?'

'There is no risk if the bidding is correct. It should be a mathematical certainty. Unfortunately, few people really bid well. They know the opening bids but later they lose their heads. They cannot distinguish between a hand with winning cards in it and a hand without losing cards – but I mustn't give you a lecture on bridge, or on the losing count, M. Poirot.'

'It would improve my play, I am sure, madame.'

Mrs Lorrimer resumed her study of the score.

'After that excitement the next hands were rather tame. Have you the fourth score there? Ah, yes. A ding-dong battle – neither side able to score below.'

'It is often like that as the evening wears on.'

'Yes, one starts tamely and then the cards get worked up.'

Poirot collected the scores and made a little bow.

'Madame, I congratulate you. Your card memory is magnificent – but magnificent! You remember, one might say, every card that was played!'

'I believe I do!'

'Memory is a wonderful gift. With it the past is never the past – I should imagine, madame, that to you the past unrolls itself, every incident clear as yesterday. Is that so?'

She looked at him quickly. Her eyes were wide and dark.

It was only for a moment, then she had resumed her woman-of-the-world manner, but Hercule Poirot did not doubt. That shot had gone home.

Mrs Lorrimer rose.

'I'm afraid I shall have to leave now. I am so sorry – but I really mustn't be late.'

'Of course not – of course not. I apologize for trespassing on your time.'

'I'm sorry I haven't been able to help you more.'

'But you have helped me,' said Hercule Poirot.

'I hardly think so.'

She spoke with decision.

'But yes. You have told me something I wanted to know.'

She asked no question as to what that something was.

He held out his hand.

'Thank you, madame, for your forbearance.'

As she shook hands with him she said:

'You are an extraordinary man, M. Poirot.'

'I am as the good God made me, madame.'

'We are all that, I suppose.'

'Not all, madame. Some of us have tried to improve on His pattern. Mr Shaitana, for instance.'

'In what way do you mean?'

'He had a very pretty taste in *objets de vertu* and *bric-à-brac* – he should have been content with that. Instead, he collected other things.'

'What sort of things?'

'Well – shall we say – sensations?'

'And don't you think that was *dans son caractère*?'

Poirot shook his head gravely.

'He played the part of the devil too successfully. But he was not the devil. *Au fond*, he was a stupid man. And so – he died.'

'Because he was stupid?'

'It is the sin that is never forgiven and always punished, madame.'

There was a silence. Then Poirot said:

'I take my departure. A thousand thanks for your amiability, madame. I will not come again unless you send for me.'

Her eyebrows rose.

'Dear me, M. Poirot, why should I send for you?'

'You might. It is just an idea. If so, I will come. Remember that.'

He bowed once more and left the room.

In the street he said to himself:

'I am right . . . I am sure I am right . . . It *must* be that!'

CHAPTER TWELVE

Anne Meredith

Mrs Oliver extricated herself from the driving-seat of her little two-seater with some difficulty. To begin with, the makers of modern motor-cars assume that only a pair of sylph-like knees will ever be under the steering wheel. It is also the fashion to sit low. That being so, for a middle-aged woman of generous proportions it requires a good deal of superhuman wriggling to get out from under the steering wheel. In the second place, the seat next to the driving-seat was encumbered by several maps, a handbag, three novels and a large bag of apples. Mrs Oliver was partial to apples and had indeed been known to eat as many as five pounds straight off whilst composing the complicated plot of *The Death in the Drain Pipe* – coming to herself with a start and an incipient stomach-ache an hour and ten minutes after she was due at an important luncheon party given in her honour.

With a final determined heave and a sharp shove with a knee against a recalcitrant door, Mrs Oliver arrived a little too suddenly on the sidewalk outside the gate of Wendon Cottage, showering apple cores freely round her as she did so.

She gave a deep sigh, pushed back her country hat to an unfashionable angle, looked down with approval at the tweeds she had remembered to put on, frowned a little when she saw that she had absent-mindedly retained her London high-heeled patent leather shoes, and pushing open the gate of Wendon Cottage walked up the flagged path to the front door. She rang the bell and executed a cheerful little rat-a-tat-tat on the knocker – a quaint conceit in the form of a toad's head.

As nothing happened she repeated the performance.

After a further pause of a minute and a half, Mrs Oliver stepped briskly round the side of the house on a voyage of exploration.

There was a small old-fashioned garden with Michaelmas daisies and straggling chrysanthemums behind the cottage, and beyond it a field. Beyond the field was the river. For an October day the sun was warm.

Two girls were just crossing the field in the direction of the cottage. As they came through the gate into the garden, the foremost of the two stopped dead.

Mrs Oliver came forward.

'How do you do, Miss Meredith? You remember me, don't you?'

'Oh – oh, of course.' Anne Meredith extended her hand hurriedly. Her eyes looked wide and startled. Then she pulled herself together.

'This is my friend who lives with me – Miss Dawes. Rhoda, this is Mrs Oliver.'

The other girl was tall, dark, and vigorous-looking. She said excitedly:

'Oh, are you the Mrs Oliver? Ariadne Oliver?'

'I am,' said Mrs Oliver, and she added to Anne, 'Now let us sit down somewhere, my dear, because I've got a lot to say to you.'

'Of course. And we'll have tea –'

'Tea can wait,' said Mrs Oliver.

Anne led the way to a little group of deck and basket chairs, all rather dilapidated. Mrs Oliver chose the strongest-looking with some care, having had various unfortunate experiences with flimsy summer furniture.

'Now, my dear,' she said briskly. 'Don't let's beat about the bush. About this murder the other evening. We've got to get busy and do something.'

'Do something?' queried Anne.

'Naturally,' said Mrs Oliver. 'I don't know what *you*

think, but I haven't the least doubt who did it. That doctor. What was his name? Roberts. That's it! Roberts. A Welsh name! I never trust the Welsh! I had a Welsh nurse and she took me to Harrogate one day and went home having forgotten all about me. Very unstable. But never mind about her. Roberts did it – that's the point and we must put our heads together and prove he did.'

Rhoda Dawes laughed suddenly – then she blushed.

'I beg your pardon. But you're – you're so different from what I would have imagined.'

'A disappointment, I expect,' said Mrs Oliver serenely. 'I'm used to that. Never mind. What we must do is prove that Roberts did it!'

'How can we?' said Anne.

'Oh, don't be so defeatist, Anne,' cried Rhoda Dawes. 'I think Mrs Oliver's splendid. Of course, she knows all about these things. She'll do just as Sven Hjerson does.'

Blushing slightly at the name of her celebrated Finnish detective, Mrs Oliver said:

'It's got to be done, and I'll tell you why, child. You don't want people thinking *you* did it?'

'Why should they?' asked Anne, her colour rising.

'You know what people are!' said Mrs Oliver. 'The three who didn't do it will come in for just as much suspicion as the one who did.'

Anne Meredith said slowly:

'I still don't quite see why you come to *me*, Mrs Oliver?'

'Because in my opinion the other two don't matter! Mrs Lorrimer is one of those women who play bridge at bridge clubs all day. Women like that *must* be made of armour-plating – they can look after themselves all right! And anyway she's old. It wouldn't matter if anyone thought she'd done it. A girl's different. She's got her life in front of her.'

'And Major Despard?' asked Anne.

'Pah!' said Mrs Oliver. 'He's a man! I never worry about men. Men can look after themselves. Do it remarkably well, if you ask me. Besides, Major Despard enjoys a dangerous life. He's getting his fun at home instead of on the Irrawaddy – or do I mean the Limpopo? You know what I mean – that yellow African river that men like so much. No, I'm not worrying my head about either of those two.'

'It's very kind of you,' said Anne slowly.

'It was a beastly thing to happen,' said Rhoda. 'It's broken Anne up, Mrs Oliver. She's awfully sensitive. And I think you're quite right. It would be ever so much better to do something than just to sit here thinking about it all.'

'Of course it would,' said Mrs Oliver. 'To tell you the truth, a real murder has never come my way before. And, to continue telling the truth, I don't believe real murder is very much in my line. I'm so used to loading the dice – if you understand what I mean. But I wasn't going to be out of it and let those three men have all the fun to themselves. I've always said that if a woman were the head of Scotland Yard –'

'Yes?' said Rhoda, leaning forward with parted lips. 'If you were head of Scotland Yard, what would you do?'

'I should arrest Dr Roberts straight away –'

'Yes?'

'However, I'm not the head of Scotland Yard,' said Mrs Oliver, retreating from dangerous ground. 'I'm a private individual –'

'Oh, you're not that,' said Rhoda, confusedly complimentary.

'Here we are,' continued Mrs Oliver, 'three private individuals – all women. Let us see what we can do by putting our heads together.'

Anne Meredith nodded thoughtfully. Then she said:

'Why do you think Dr Roberts did it?'

'He's that sort of man,' replied Mrs Oliver promptly.

'Don't you think, though –' Anne hesitated. 'Wouldn't a doctor –? I mean something like poison would be so much easier for him.'

'Not at all. Poison – drugs of any kind would point straight to a doctor. Look how they are always leaving cases of dangerous drugs in cars all over London and getting them stolen. No, just because he *was* a doctor he'd take special care not to use anything of a medical kind.'

'I see,' said Anne doubtfully.

Then she said:

'But why do you think he wanted to kill Mr Shaitana? Have you any idea?'

'Idea? I've got any amount of ideas. In fact, that's just the difficulty. It always is my difficulty. I can never think of even one plot at a time. I always think of at least five, and it's agony to decide between them. I can think of six beautiful reasons for the murder. The trouble is I've no earthly means of knowing which is right. To begin with, perhaps Shaitana was a moneylender. He had a very oily look. Roberts was in his clutches, and killed him because he couldn't get the money to repay the loan. Or perhaps Shaitana ruined his daughter or his sister. Or perhaps Roberts is a bigamist, and Shaitana knew it. Or possibly Roberts married Shaitana's second cousin, and will inherit all Shaitana's money through her. Or – How many have I got to?'

'Four,' said Rhoda.

'Or – and this is a really good one – suppose Shaitana knew some secret in Roberts' past. Perhaps you didn't notice, my dear, but Shaitana said something rather peculiar at dinner – just before a rather queer pause.'

Anne stooped to tickle a caterpillar. She said, 'I don't think I remember.'

'What did he say?' asked Rhoda.

'Something about – what was it? – an accident and poison. Don't you remember?'

Anne's left hand tightened on the basketwork of her chair.

'I do remember something of the kind,' she said composedly.

Rhoda said suddenly, 'Darling, you ought to have a coat. It's not summer, remember. Go and get one.'

Anne shook her head.

'I'm quite warm.'

But she gave a queer little shiver as she spoke.

'You see my theory,' went on Mrs Oliver. 'I dare say one of the doctor's patients poisoned himself by accident; but, of course, really, it was the doctor's own doing. I dare say he's murdered lots of people that way.'

A sudden colour came into Anne's cheeks. She said, 'Do doctors usually want to murder their patients wholesale? Wouldn't it have rather a regrettable effect on their practice?'

'There would be a reason, of course,' said Mrs Oliver vaguely.

'I think the idea is absurd,' said Anne crisply. 'Absolutely absurdly melodramatic.'

'Oh, Anne!' cried Rhoda in an agony of apology. She looked at Mrs Oliver. Her eyes, rather like those of an intelligent spaniel, seemed to be trying to say something. 'Try and understand. Try and understand,' those eyes said.

'I think it's a splendid idea, Mrs Oliver,' Rhoda said earnestly. 'And a doctor could get hold of something quite untraceable, couldn't he?'

'Oh!' exclaimed Anne.

The other two turned to look at her.

'I remember something else,' she said. 'Mr Shaitana said something about a doctor's opportunities in a laboratory. He must have meant something by that.'

'It wasn't Mr Shaitana who said that.' Mrs Oliver shook her head. 'It was Major Despard.'

A footfall on the garden walk made her turn her head. 'Well!' she exclaimed. 'Talk of the devil!'

Major Despard had just come round the corner of the house.

CHAPTER THIRTEEN

Second Visitor

At the sight of Mrs Oliver, Major Despard looked slightly taken aback. Under his tan his face flushed a rich brick red. Embarrassment made him jerky. He made for Anne.

'I apologize, Miss Meredith,' he said. 'Been ringing your bell. Nothing happened. Was passing this way. Thought I might just look you up.'

'I'm so sorry you've been ringing,' said Anne. 'We haven't got a maid – only a woman who comes in the mornings.'

She introduced him to Rhoda.

Rhoda said briskly:

'Let's have some tea. It's getting chilly. We'd better go in.'

They all went into the house. Rhoda disappeared into the kitchen. Mrs Oliver said:

'This is quite a coincidence – our all meeting here.'

Despard said slowly, 'Yes.'

His eyes rested on her thoughtfully – appraising eyes.

'I've been telling Miss Meredith,' said Mrs Oliver, who was thoroughly enjoying herself, 'that we ought to have a plan of campaign. About the murder, I mean. Of course, that doctor did it. Don't you agree with me?'

'Couldn't say. Very little to go on.'

Mrs Oliver put on her 'How like a man!' expression.

A certain air of constraint had settled over the three. Mrs Oliver sensed it quickly enough. When Rhoda brought in tea she rose and said she must be getting back to town. No, it was ever so kind of them, but she wouldn't have any tea.

'I'm going to leave you my card,' she said. 'Here it is, with my address on it. Come and see me when you come up to town, and we'll talk everything over and see if we can't think of something ingenious to get to the bottom of things.'

'I'll come out to the gate with you,' said Rhoda.

Just as they were walking down the path to the front gate, Anne Meredith ran out of the house and overtook them.

'I've been thinking things over,' she said.

Her pale face looked unusually resolute.

'Yes, my dear?'

'It's extraordinarily kind of you, Mrs Oliver, to have taken all this trouble. But I'd really rather not do anything at all. I mean – it was all so horrible. I just want to forget about it.'

'My dear child, the question is, will you be *allowed* to forget about it?'

'Oh, I quite understand that the police won't let it drop. They'll probably come here and ask me a lot more questions. I'm prepared for that. But privately, I mean, I don't want to think about it – or be reminded of it in any way. I dare say I'm a coward, but that's how I feel about it.'

'Oh, Anne!' cried Rhoda Dawes.

'I can understand your feeling, but I'm not at all sure that you're wise,' said Mrs Oliver. 'Left to themselves, the police will probably never find out the truth.'

Anne Meredith shrugged her shoulders.

'Does that really matter?'

'Matter?' cried Rhoda. 'Of course it matters. It *does* matter, doesn't it, Mrs Oliver?'

'I should certainly say so,' said Mrs Oliver dryly.

'I don't agree,' said Anne obstinately. 'Nobody who knows me would ever think I'd done it. I don't see any reason for interfering. It's the business of the police to get at the truth.'

'Oh, Anne, you *are* spiritless,' said Rhoda.

'That's how I feel, anyway,' said Anne. She held out her hand. 'Thank you very much, Mrs Oliver. It's very good of you to have bothered.'

'Of course, if you feel that way, there's nothing more to be said,' said Mrs Oliver cheerfully. 'I, at any rate, shall not let the grass grow under my feet. Goodbye, my dear. Look me up in London if you change your mind.'

She climbed into the car, started it, and drove off, waving a cheerful hand at the two girls.

Rhoda suddenly made a dash after the car and leapt on the running-board.

'What you said – about looking you up in London,' she said breathlessly. 'Did you only mean Anne, or did you mean me, too?'

Mrs Oliver applied the brake.

'I meant both of you, of course.'

'Oh, thank you. Don't stop. I – perhaps I might come one day. There's something – No, don't stop. I can jump off.'

She did so and, waving a hand, ran back to the gate, where Anne was standing.

'What on earth – ?' began Anne.

'Isn't she a duck?' asked Rhoda enthusiastically. 'I do like her. She had on odd stockings, did you notice? I'm sure she's frightfully clever. She must be – to write all those books. What fun if she found out the truth when the police and everyone were baffled.'

'Why did she come here?' asked Anne.

Rhoda's eyes opened wide.

'Darling – she told you –'

Anne made an impatient gesture.

'We must go in. I forgot. I've left him all alone.'

'Major Despard? Anne, he's frightfully good-looking, isn't he?'

'I suppose he is.'

They walked up the path together.

Major Despard was standing by the mantelpiece, tea-cup in hand.

He cut short Anne's apologies for leaving him.

'Miss Meredith, I want to explain why I've butted in like this.'

'Oh – but –'

'I said that I happened to be passing – that wasn't strictly true. I came here on purpose.'

'How did you know my address?' asked Anne slowly.

'I got it from Superintendent Battle.'

He saw her shrink slightly at the name.

He went on quickly:

'Battle's on his way here now. I happened to see him at Paddington. I got my car out and came down here. I knew I could beat the train easily.'

'But why?'

Despard hesitated just a minute.

'I may have been presumptuous – but I had the impression that you were, perhaps, what is called "alone in the world".'

'She's got me,' said Rhoda.

Despard shot a quick glance at her, rather liking the gallant boyish figure that leant against the mantlepiece and was following his words so intensely. They were an attractive pair, these two.

'I'm sure she couldn't have a more devoted friend than you, Miss Dawes,' he said courteously; 'but it occurred to me that, in the peculiar circumstances, the advice of some one with a good dash of world wisdom might not be amiss. Frankly, the situation is this: Miss Meredith is under suspicion of having committed murder. The same thing applies to me and to the two other people who were in the room last night. Such a situation is not agreeable – and it has its own peculiar difficulties and dangers which some one as young and inexperienced as you are, Miss Meredith, might not recognize. In my opinion, you ought to put yourself in the hands of a thoroughly good solicitor. Perhaps you have already done so?'

Anne Meredith shook her head.

'I never thought of it.'

'Exactly as I suspected. Have you got a good man – a London man, for choice?'

Again Anne shook her head.

'I've hardly ever needed a solicitor.'

'There's Mr Bury,' said Rhoda. 'But he's about a hundred-and-two, and quite gaga.'

'If you'll allow me to advise you, Miss Meredith, I recommend your going to Mr Myherne, my own solicitor. Jacobs, Peel & Jacobs is the actual name of the firm. They're first-class people, and they know all the ropes.'

Anne had got paler. She sat down.

'Is it really necessary?' she asked in a low voice.

'I should say emphatically so. There are all sorts of legal pitfalls.'

'Are these people very – expensive?'

'That doesn't matter a bit,' said Rhoda. 'That will be *quite* all right, Major Despard. I think everything you say is quite true. Anne ought to be protected.'

'Their charges will, I think, be quite reasonable,' said Despard. He added seriously: 'I really do think it's a wise course, Miss Meredith.'

'Very well,' said Anne slowly. 'I'll do it if you think so.'

'Good.'

Rhoda said warmly.

'I think it's awfully nice of you, Major Despard. Really frightfully nice.'

Anne said, 'Thank you.'

She hesitated, and then said:

'Did you say Superintendent Battle was coming here?'

'Yes. You mustn't be alarmed by that. It's inevitable.'

'Oh, I know. As a matter of fact, I've been expecting him.'

Rhoda said impulsively:

'Poor darling – it's nearly killing her, this business. It's such a shame – so frightfully unfair.'

Despard said:

'I agree – it's a pretty beastly business – dragging a young girl into an affair of this kind. If anyone wanted to stick a knife into Shaitana, they ought to have chosen some other place or time.'

Rhoda asked squarely:

'Who do you think did it? Dr Roberts or that Mrs Lorrimer?'

A very faint smile stirred Despard's moustache.

'May have done it myself, for all you know.'

'Oh, no,' cried Rhoda. 'Anne and I know *you* didn't do it.'

He looked at them both with kindly eyes.

A nice pair of kids. Touchingly full of faith and trust. A timid little creature, the Meredith girl. Never mind, Myherne would see her through. The other was a fighter. He doubted if she would have crumpled up in the same way if she'd been in her friend's place. Nice girls. He'd like to know more about them.

These thoughts passed through his mind. Aloud he said:

'Never take anything for granted, Miss Dawes. I don't set as much value on human life as most people do. All this hysterical fuss about road deaths, for instance. Man is always in danger – from traffic, from germs, from a hundred-and-one things. As well be killed one way as another. The moment you begin being careful of yourself – adopting as your motto "Safety First" – you might as well be dead, in my opinion.'

'Oh, I do agree with you,' cried Rhoda. 'I think one ought to live frightfully dangerously – if one gets the chance that is. But life, on the whole, is terribly tame.'

'It has its moments.'

'Yes, for *you*. You go to out-of-the-way places and get

mauled by tigers and shoot things and jiggers bury themselves in your toes and insects sting you, and everything's terribly uncomfortable but frightfully thrilling.'

'Well, Miss Meredith has had her thrill, too. I don't suppose it often happens that you've actually *been in the room* while a murder was committed –'

'Oh, don't!' cried Anne.

He said quickly:

'I'm sorry.'

But Rhoda said with a sigh:

'Of course it was awful – but it was exciting, too! I don't think Anne appreciates that side of it. You know, I think that Mrs Oliver is thrilled to the core to have been there that night.'

'Mrs –? Oh, your fat friend who writes the books about the unpronounceable Finn. Is she trying her hand at detection in real life?'

'She wants to.'

'Well, let's wish her luck. It would be amusing if she put one over on Battle and Co.'

'What is Superintendent Battle like?' asked Rhoda curiously.

Major Despard said gravely:

'He's an extraordinarily astute man. A man of remarkable ability.'

'Oh!' said Rhoda. 'Anne said he looked rather stupid.'

'That, I should imagine, is part of Battle's stock-in-trade. But we mustn't make any mistakes. Battle's no fool.'

He rose.

'Well, I must be off. There's just one other thing I'd like to say.'

Anne had risen also.

'Yes?' she said, as she held out her hand.

Despard paused a minute, picking his words carefully. He took her hand and retained it in his. He looked straight into the wide, beautiful grey eyes.

'Don't be offended with me,' he said. 'I just want to say this: It's humanly possible that there may be some feature of your acqaintanceship with Shaitana that you don't want to come out. If so – don't be angry, please' (he felt the instinctive pull of her hand) – 'you are perfectly within your rights in refusing to answer any questions Battle may ask unless your solicitor is present.'

Anne tore her hand away. Her eyes opened, their grey darkening with anger.

'There's nothing – *nothing* . . . I hardly knew the beastly man.'

'Sorry,' said Major Despard. 'Thought I ought to mention it.'

'It's quite true,' said Rhoda. 'Anne barely knew him. She didn't like him much, but he gave frightfully good parties.'

'That,' said Major Despard grimly, 'seems to have been the only justification for the late Mr Shaitana's existence.'

Anne said in a cold voice:

'Superintendent Battle can ask me anything he likes. I've nothing to hide – *nothing.*'

Despard said very gently, 'Please forgive me.'

She looked at him. Her anger dwindled. She smiled – it was a very sweet smile.'

'It's all right,' she said. 'You meant it kindly, I know.'

She held out her hand again. He took it and said:

'We're in the same boat, you know. We ought to be pals . . .'

It was Anne who went with him to the gate. When she came back Rhoda was staring out of the window and whistling. She turned as her friend entered the room.

'He's frightfully attractive, Anne.'

'He's nice, isn't he?'

'A great deal more than nice . . . I've got an absolute passion for him. Why wasn't I at that damned dinner instead of you? I'd have enjoyed the excitement – the net closing round me – the shadow of the scaffold –'

'No, you wouldn't. You're talking nonsense, Rhoda.'
Anne's voice was sharp. Then it softened as she said:

'It was nice of him to come all this way – for a stranger – a girl he's only met once.'

'Oh, he fell for you. Obviously. Men don't do purely disinterested kindnesses. He wouldn't have come toddling down if you'd been cross-eyed and covered with pimples.'

'Don't you think so?'

'I do not, my good idiot. Mrs Oliver's a *much* more disinterested party.'

'I don't like her,' said Anne abruptly. 'I had a sort of feeling about her . . . I wonder what she really came for?'

'The usual suspicions of your own sex. I dare say Major Despard had an axe to grind if it comes to that.'

'I'm sure he hadn't,' cried Anne hotly.

Then she blushed as Rhoda Dawes laughed.

CHAPTER FOURTEEN

Third Visitor

Superintendent Battle arrived at Wallingford about six o'clock. It was his intention to learn as much as he could from innocent local gossip before interviewing Miss Anne Meredith.

It was not difficult to glean such information as there was. Without committing himself definitely to any statement, the superintendent nevertheless gave several different impressions of his rank and calling in life.

At least two people would have said confidently that he was a London builder come down to see about a new wing to be added to the cottage, from another you would have learned that he was 'one of these weekenders wanting to take a furnished cottage,' and two more would have said they knew positively, and for a fact, that he was a representative of a hard-court tennis firm.

The information that the superintendent gathered was entirely favourable.

'Wendon Cottage – Yes, that's right – on the Marlbury Road. You can't miss it. Yes, two young ladies. Miss Dawes and Miss Meredith. Very nice young ladies, too. The quiet kind.

'Here for years? Oh, no, not that long. Just over two years. September quarter they come in. Mr Pickersgill they bought it from. Never used it much, he didn't, after his wife died.'

Superintendent Battle's informant had never heard they came from Northumberland. London, *he* thought they came from. Popular in the neighbourhood, though some people were old-fashioned and didn't think two young ladies ought to be living alone. But very quiet, they were.

None of this cocktail-drinking weekend lot. Miss Rhoda, she was the dashing one. Miss Meredith was the quiet one. Yes, it was Miss Dawes what paid the bills. She was the one had got the money.

The superintendent's researches at last led him inevitably to Mrs Astwell – who 'did' for the ladies at Wendon Cottage.

Mrs Astwell was a locquacious lady.

'Well, no, sir. I hardly think they'd want to sell. Not so soon. They only got in two years ago. I've done for them from the beginning, yes, sir. Eight o'clock till twelve – those are my hours. Very nice, lively young ladies, always ready for a joke or a bit of fun. Not stuck up at all.

'Well, of course, I couldn't say if it's the same Miss Dawes *you* knew, sir – the same *family*, I mean. It's my fancy her home's in Devonshire. She gets the cream sent her now and again, and says it reminds her of home; so I think it must be.

'As you say, sir, it's sad for so many young ladies having to earn their living nowadays. These young ladies aren't what you'd call rich, but they have a very pleasant life. It's Miss Dawes has got the money, of course. Miss Anne's her companion, in a manner of speaking, I suppose you might say. The cottage belongs to Miss Dawes.

'I couldn't really say what part Miss Anne comes from. I've heard her mention the Isle of Wight, and I know she doesn't like the North of England; and she and Miss Rhoda were together in Devonshire, because I've heard them joke about the hills and talk about the pretty coves and beaches.'

The flow went on. Every now and then Superintendent Battle made a mental note. Later, a cryptic word or two was jotted down in his little book.

At half-past eight that evening he walked up the path to the door of Wendon Cottage.

It was opened to him by a tall, dark girl wearing a frock of orange cretonne.

'Miss Meredith live here?' inquired Superintendent Battle.

He looked very wooden and soldierly.

'Yes, she does.'

'I'd like to speak to her, please. Superintendent Battle.'

He was immediately favoured with a piercing stare.

'Come in,' said Rhoda Dawes, drawing back from the doorway.

Anne Meredith was sitting in a cosy chair by the fire, sipping coffee. She was wearing embroidered crêpe-de-chine pyjamas.

'It's Superintendent Battle,' said Rhoda, ushering in the guest.

Anne rose and came forward with outstretched hand.

'A bit late for a call,' said Battle. 'But I wanted to find you in, and it's been a fine day.'

Anne smiled.

'Will you have some coffee, Superintendent? Rhoda, fetch another cup.'

'Well, it's very kind of you, Miss Meredith.'

'We think we make rather good coffee,' said Anne.

She indicated a chair, and Superintendent Battle sat down. Rhoda brought a cup, and Anne poured out his coffee. The fire crackled and the flowers in the vases made an agreeable impression upon the superintendent.

It was a pleasant homey atmosphere. Anne seemed self-possessed and at her ease, and the other girl continued to stare at him with devouring interest.

'We've been expecting you,' said Anne.

Her tone was almost reproachful. 'Why have you neglected me?' it seemed to say.

'Sorry, Miss Meredith. I've had a lot of routine work to do.'

'Satisfactory?'

'Not particularly. But it all has to be done. I've turned Dr Roberts inside out, so to speak. And the same for Mrs Lorrimer. And now I've come to do the same for you, Miss Meredith.'

Anne smiled.

'I'm ready.'

'What about Major Despard?' asked Rhoda.

'Oh, he won't be overlooked. I can promise you that,' said Battle.

He set down his coffee-cup and looked towards Anne. She sat up a little straighter in her chair.

'I'm quite ready, superintendent. What do you want to know?'

'Well, roughly, all about yourself, Miss Meredith.'

'I'm quite a respectable person,' said Anne, smiling.

'She's led a blameless life, too,' said Rhoda. 'I can answer for that.'

'Well, that's very nice,' said Superintendent Battle cheerfully. 'You've known Miss Meredith a long time, then?'

'We were at school together,' said Rhoda. 'What ages ago, it seems, doesn't it, Anne?'

'So long ago, you can hardly remember it, I suppose,' said Battle with a chuckle. 'Now, then, Miss Meredith, I'm afraid I'm going to be rather like those forms you fill up for passports.'

'I was born –' began Anne.

'Of poor but honest parents,' Rhoda put in.

Superintendent Battle held up a slightly reproving hand.

'Now, now, young lady,' he said.

'Rhoda, darling,' said Anne gravely. 'It's serious, this.'

'Sorry,' said Rhoda.

'Now, Miss Meredith, you were born – where?'

'At Quetta, in India.'

'Ah, yes. Your people were Army folk?'

'Yes – my father was Major John Meredith. My mother died when I was eleven. Father retired when I was fifteen

110

and went to live in Cheltenham. He died when I was eighteen and left practically no money.'

Battle nodded his head sympathetically.

'Bit of a shock to you, I expect.'

'It was, rather. I always knew that we weren't well off, but to find there was practically nothing – well, that's different.'

'What did you do, Miss Meredith?'

'I had to take a job. I hadn't been particularly well educated and I wasn't clever. I didn't know typing or shorthand, or anything. A friend in Cheltenham found me a job with friends of hers – two small boys home in the holidays, and general help in the house.'

'Name, please?'

'That was Mrs Eldon, The Larches, Ventnor. I stayed there for two years, and then the Eldons went abroad. Then I went to a Mrs Deering.'

'My aunt,' put in Rhoda.

'Yes, Rhoda got me the job. I was very happy. Rhoda used to come and stay sometimes, and we had great fun.'

'What were you there – companion?'

'Yes – it amounted to that.'

'More like under-gardener,' said Rhoda.

She explained:

'My Aunt Emily is just mad on gardening. Anne spent most of her time weeding or putting in bulbs.'

'And you left Mrs Deering?'

'Her health got worse, and she had to have a regular nurse.'

'She's got cancer,' said Rhoda. 'Poor darling, she has to have morphia and things like that.'

'She had been very kind to me. I was very sorry to go,' went on Anne.

'I was looking about for a cottage,' said Rhoda, 'and wanting some one to share it with me. Daddy's married

111

again – not my sort at all. I asked Anne to come here with me, and she's been here ever since.'

'Well, that certainly seems a most blameless life,' said Battle. 'Let's just get the dates clear. You were with Mrs Eldon two years, you say. By the way, what is her address now?'

'She's in Palestine. Her husband has some Government appointment out there – I'm not sure what.'

'Ah, well, I can soon find out. And after that you went to Mrs Deering?'

'I was with her three years,' said Anne quickly. 'Her address is Marsh Dene, Little Hembury, Devon.'

'I see,' said Battle. 'So you are now twenty-five, Miss Meredith. Now, there's just one thing more – the name and address of a couple of people in Cheltenham who knew you and your father.'

Anne supplied him with these.

'Now, about this trip to Switzerland – where you met Mr Shaitana. Did you go alone there – or was Miss Dawes here with you?'

'We went out together. We joined some other people. There was a party of eight.'

'Tell me about your meeting with Mr Shaitana.'

Anne crinkled her brows.

'There's really nothing to tell. He was just there. We knew him in the way you know people in a hotel. He got first prize at the fancy dress ball. He went as Mephistopheles.'

Superintendent Battle sighed.

'Yes, that always was his favourite effect.'

'He really was marvellous,' said Rhoda. 'He hardly had to make up at all.'

The superintendent looked from one girl to the other.

'Which of you two young ladies knew him best?'

Anne hesitated. It was Rhoda who answered.

'Both the same to begin with. Awfully little, that is. You

see, our crowd was the ski-ing lot, and we were off doing runs most days and dancing together in the evenings. But then Shaitana seemed to take rather a fancy to Anne. You know, went out of his way to pay her compliments, and all that. We ragged her about it, rather.'

'I just think he did it to annoy me,' said Anne. 'Because I didn't like him. I think it amused him to make me feel embarrassed.'

Rhoda said laughing:

'We told Anne it would be a nice rich marriage for her. She got simply wild with us.'

'Perhaps,' said Battle, 'you'd give me the names of the other people in your party?'

'You aren't what I call a trustful man,' said Rhoda. 'Do you think that every word we're telling you is downright lies?'

Superintendent Battle twinkled.

'I'm going to make sure it isn't, anyway,' he said.

'You *are* suspicious,' said Rhoda.

She scribbled some names on a piece of paper and gave it to him.

Battle rose.

'Well, thank you very much, Miss Meredith,' he said. 'As Miss Dawes says, you seem to have led a particularly blameless life. I don't think you need worry much. It's odd the way Mr Shaitana's manner changed to you. You'll excuse my asking, but he didn't ask you to marry him – or – er – pester you with attentions of another kind?'

'He didn't try to seduce her,' said Rhoda helpfully. 'If that's what you mean.'

Anne was blushing.

'Nothing of the kind,' she said. 'He was always most polite and – and – formal. It was just his elaborate manners that made me uncomfortable.'

'And little things he said or hinted?'

'Yes – at least – no. He never hinted things.'

'Sorry. These lady-killers do sometimes. Well, good-night, Miss Meredith. Thank you very much. Excellent coffee. Goodnight, Miss Dawes.'

'There,' said Rhoda as Anne came back into the room after shutting the door after Battle. 'That's over, and not so very terrible. He's a nice fatherly man, and he evidently doesn't suspect you in the least. It was all ever so much better than I expected.'

Anne sank down with a sigh.

'It was really quite easy,' she said. 'It was silly of me to work myself up so. I thought he'd try to browbeat me – like K.C.s on the stage.'

'He looks sensible,' said Rhoda. 'He'd know well enough you're not a murdering kind of female.'

She hesitated and then said:

'I say, Anne, you didn't mention being at Croftways. Did you forget?'

Anne said slowly:

'I didn't think it counted. I was only there a few months. And there's no one to ask about me there. I can write and tell him if you think it matters; but I'm sure it doesn't. Let's leave it.'

'Right, if you say so.'

Rhoda rose and turned on the wireless.

A raucous voice said:

'You have just heard the Black Nubians play "Why do you tell me lies, Baby?"'

CHAPTER FIFTEEN

Major Despard

Major Despard came out of the Albany, turned sharply into Regent Street and jumped on a bus.

It was the quiet time of day – the top of the bus had very few seats occupied. Despard made his way forward and sat down on the front seat.

He had jumped on the bus while it was going. Now it came to a halt, took up passengers and made its way once more up Regent Street.

A second traveller climbed the steps, made his way forward and sat down in the front seat on the other side.

Despard did not notice the newcomer, but after a few minutes a tentative voice murmured:

'It is a good view of London, is it not, that one gets from the top of a bus?'

Despard turned his head. He looked puzzled for a moment, then his face cleared.

'I beg your pardon, M. Poirot. I didn't see it was you. Yes as you say, one has a good bird's eye view of the world from here. It was better, though, in the old days, when there wasn't all this caged-in glass business.'

Poirot sighed.

'*Tout de même*, it was not always agreeable in the wet weather when the inside was full. And there is much wet weather in this country.'

'Rain? Rain never did any harm to anyone.'

'You are in error,' said Poirot. 'It leads often to a *fluxion de poitrine*.'

Despard smiled.

'I see you belong to the well-wrapped-up school, M. Poirot.'

Poirot was indeed well equipped against any treachery of an autumn day. He wore a greatcoat and a muffler.

'Rather odd, running into you like this,' said Despard.

He did not see the smile that the muffler concealed. There was nothing odd in this encounter. Having ascertained a likely hour for Despard to leave his rooms, Poirot had been waiting for him. He had prudently not risked leaping on the bus, but he had trotted after it to its next stopping-place and boarded it there.

'True. We have not seen each other since the evening at Mr Shaitana's,' he replied.

'Aren't you taking a hand in the business?' asked Despard.

Poirot scratched his ear delicately.

'I reflect,' he said. 'I reflect a good deal. To run to and fro, to make the investigations, that, no. It does not suit my age, my temperament, or my figure.'

Despard said unexpectedly:

'Reflect, eh? Well, you might do worse. There's too much rushing about nowadays. If people sat tight and thought about a thing before they tackled it, there'd be less mess-ups than there are.'

'Is that your procedure in life, Major Despard?'

'Usually,' said the other simply. 'Get your bearings, figure out your route, weigh up the pros and cons, make your decision – stick to it.'

His mouth set grimly.

'And, after that, nothing will turn you from your path, eh?' asked Poirot.

'Oh, I don't say that. No use in being pig-headed over things. If you've made a mistake, admit it.'

'But I imagine that you do not often make a mistake, Major Despard.'

'We all make mistakes, M. Poirot.'

'Some of us,' said Poirot with a certain coldness, possibly due to the pronoun the other had used, 'make less than others.'

Despard looked at him, smiled slightly and said:

'Don't you ever have a failure, M. Poirot?'

'The last time was twenty-eight years ago,' said Poirot with dignity. 'And even then, there were circumstances – but no matter.'

'That seems a pretty good record,' said Despard.

He added: 'What about Shaitana's death? That doesn't count, I suppose, since it isn't officially your business.'

'It is not my business – no. But, all the same, it offends my *amour propre*. I consider it an impertinence, you comprehend, for a murder to be committed under my very nose – by some one who mocks himself at my ability to solve it!'

'Not under *your* nose only,' said Despard drily. 'Under the nose of the Criminal Investigation Department also.'

'That was probably a bad mistake,' said Poirot gravely. 'The good Superintendent Battle, he may look wooden, but he is not wooden in the head – not at all.'

'I agree,' said Despard. 'That stolidity is a pose. He's a very clever and able officer.'

'And I think he is very active in the case.'

'Oh, he's active enough. See a nice quiet soldierly-looking fellow on one of the back seats?'

Poirot looked over his shoulder.

'There is no one here now but ourselves.'

'Oh, well, he's inside, then. He never loses me. Very efficient fellow. Varies his appearance, too, from time to time. Quite artistic about it.'

'Ah, but that would not deceive you. You have the very quick and accurate eye.'

'I never forget a face – even a black one – and that's a lot more than most people can say.'

'You are just the person I need,' said Poirot. 'What a chance, meeting you today! I need some one with a good eye and a good memory. *Malheureusement* the two seldom go together. I have asked the Dr Roberts a question, without result, and the same with Madame Lorrimer. Now, I will

117

try you and see if I get what I want. Cast your mind back to the room in which you played cards at Mr Shaitana's, and tell me what you remember of it.'

Despard looked puzzled.

'I don't quite understand.'

'Give me a description of the room – the furnishings – the objects in it.'

'I don't know that I'm much of a hand at that sort of thing,' said Despard slowly. 'It was a rotten sort of room – to my mind. Not a man's room at all. A lot of brocade and silk and stuff. Sort of room a fellow like Shaitana would have.'

'But to particularize –'

Despard shook his head.

'Afraid I didn't notice . . . He'd got some good rugs. Two Bokharas and three or four really good Persian ones, including a Hamadan and a Tabriz. Rather a good eland head – no, that was in the hall. From Rowland Ward's, I expect.'

'You do not think that the late Mr Shaitana was one to go out and shoot wild beasts?'

'Not he. Never potted anything but sitting game, I'll bet. What else was there? I'm sorry to fail you, but I really can't help much. Any amount of knick-knacks lying about. Tables were thick with them. Only thing I noticed was a rather jolly idol. Easter Island, I should say. Highly polished wood. You don't see many of them. There was some Malay stuff, too. No, I'm afraid I can't help you.'

'No matter,' said Poirot, looking slightly crestfallen.

He went on:

'Do you know, Mrs Lorrimer, she has the most amazing card memory! She could tell me the bidding and play of nearly every hand. It was astonishing.'

Despard shrugged his shoulders.

'Some women are like that. Because they play pretty well all day long, I suppose.'

'You could not do it, eh?'

The other shook his head.

'I just remember a couple of hands. One where I could have got game in diamonds – and Roberts bluffed me out of it. Went down himself, but we didn't double him, worse luck. I remember a no trumper, too. Tricky business – every card wrong. We went down a couple – lucky not to have gone down more.'

'Do you play much bridge, Major Despard?'

'No, I'm not a regular player. It's a good game, though.'

'You prefer it to poker?'

'I do personally. Poker's too much of a gamble.'

Poirot said thoughtfully:

'I do not think Mr Shaitana played any game – any card game, that is.'

'There's only one game that Shaitana played consistently,' said Despard grimly.

'And that?'

'A lowdown game.'

Poirot was silent for a minute, then he said:

'Is it that you *know* that? Or do you just *think* it?'

Despard went brick red.

'Meaning one oughtn't to say things without giving chapter and verse? I suppose that's true. Well, it's accurate enough. I happen to *know*. On the other hand, I'm not prepared to give chapter and verse. Such information as I've got came to me privately.'

'Meaning a woman or women are concerned?'

'Yes. Shaitana, like the dirty dog he was, preferred to deal with women.'

'You think he was a blackmailer? That is interesting.'

Despard shook his head.

'No, no, you've misunderstood me. In a way, Shaitana was a blackmailer, but not the common or garden sort. He wasn't after money. He was a spiritual blackmailer, if there can be such a thing.'

'And he got out of it – what?'

'He got a kick out of it. That's the only way I can put it. He got a thrill out of seeing people quail and flinch. I suppose it made him feel less of a louse and more of a man. And it's a very effective pose with women. He'd only got to hint that he knew everything – and they'd start telling him a lot of things that perhaps he didn't know. That would tickle his sense of humour. Then he'd strut about in his Mephistophelian attitude of "I know everything! I am the great Shaitana!" The man was an ape!'

'So you think that he frightened Miss Meredith that way,' said Poirot slowly.

'Miss Meredith?' Despard stared. 'I wasn't thinking of her. She isn't the kind to be afraid of a man like Shaitana.'

'*Pardon.* You meant Mrs Lorrimer.'

'No, no, no. You misunderstand me. I was speaking generally. It wouldn't be easy to frighten Mrs Lorrimer. And she's not the kind of woman who you can imagine having a guilty secret. No, I was not thinking of anyone in particular.'

'It was the general method to which you referred?'

'Exactly.'

'There is no doubt,' said Poirot slowly, 'that what you call a Dago often has a very clever understanding of women. He knows how to approach them. He worms secrets out of them –'

He paused.

Despard broke in impatiently:

'It's absurd. The man was a mountebank – nothing really dangerous about him. And yet women were afraid of him. Ridiculously so.'

He started up suddenly.

'Hallo, I've overshot the mark. Got too interested in what we were discussing. Goodbye, M. Poirot. Look down and you'll see my faithful shadow leave the bus when I do.'

He hurried to the back and down the steps. The conductor's bell jangled. But a double pull sounded before it had time to stop.

Looking down to the street below, Poirot noticed Despard striding back along the pavement. He did not trouble to pick out the following figure. Something else was interesting him.

'No one in particular,' he murmured to himself. 'Now, I wonder.'

CHAPTER SIXTEEN

The Evidence of Elsie Batt

Sergeant O'Connor was unkindly nicknamed by his colleagues at the Yard: 'The Maidservant's Prayer.'

There was no doubt that he was an extremely handsome man. Tall, erect, broad-shouldered, it was less the regularity of his features than the roguish and daredevil spark in his eye which made him so irresistible to the fair sex. It was indubitable that Sergeant O'Connor got results, and got them quickly.

So rapid was he, that only four days after the murder of Mr Shaitana, Sergeant O'Connor was sitting in the three-and-sixpenny seats at the *Willy Nilly Revue* side by side with Miss Elsie Batt, late parlourmaid to Mrs Craddock of 117 North Audley Street.

Having laid his line of approach carefully, Sergeant O'Connor was just launching the great offensive.

' – Reminds me,' he was saying, 'of the way one of my old governors used to carry on. Name of Craddock. He was an old cuss, if you like.'

'Craddock,' said Elsie. 'I was with some Craddocks once.'

'Well, that's funny. Wonder whether they were the same?'

'Lived in North Audley Street, they did,' said Elsie.

'My lot were going to London when I left them,' said O'Connor promptly. 'Yes, I believe it *was* North Audley Street. Mrs Craddock was rather a one for the gents.'

Elsie tossed her head.

'I'd no patience with her. Always finding fault and grumbling. Nothing you did right.'

'Her husband got some of it, too, didn't he?'

'She was always complaining he neglected her – that he didn't understand her. And she was always saying how bad her health was and gasping and groaning. Not ill at all, if you ask *me*.'

O'Connor slapped his knee.

'Got it. Wasn't there something about her and some doctor? A bit too thick or something?'

'You mean Dr Roberts? He was a nice gentleman, he was.'

'You girls, you're all alike,' said Sergeant O'Connor. 'The moment a man's a bad lot, all the girls stick up for him. I know his kind.'

'No, you don't, and you're all wrong about him. There wasn't anything of that kind about him. Wasn't his fault, was it, if Mrs Craddock was always sending for him? What's a doctor to do? If you ask me, he didn't think nothing of her at all, except as a patient. It was all her doing. Wouldn't leave him alone, she wouldn't.'

'That's all very well, Elsie. Don't mind me calling you Elsie, do you? Feel as though I'd known you all my life.'

'Well, you haven't! Elsie, indeed.'

She tossed her head.

'Oh, very well, Miss Batt.' He gave her a glance. 'As I was saying, that's all very well, but the husband, he cut up rough, all the same, didn't he?'

'He was a bit ratty one day,' admitted Elsie. 'But, if you ask me, he was ill at the time. He died just after, you know.'

'I remember – died of something queer, didn't he?'

'Something Japanese, it was – all from a new shaving brush, he'd got. Seems awful, doesn't it, that they're not more careful? I've not fancied anything Japanese since.'

'Buy British, that's my motto,' said Sergeant O'Connor sententiously. 'And you were saying he and the doctor had a row?'

Elsie nodded, enjoying herself as she re-lived past scandals.

'Hammer and tongs, they went at it,' she said. 'At least, the master did. Dr Roberts was ever so quiet. Just said, "Nonsense." And, "What have you got into your head?"'

'This was at the house, I suppose?'

'Yes. She'd sent for him. And then she and the master had words, and in the middle of it Dr Roberts arrived, and the master went for him.'

'What did he say exactly?'

'Well, of course, I wasn't supposed to hear. It was all in the Missus's bedroom. I thought something was up, so I got the dustpan and did the stairs. I wasn't going to miss anything.'

Sergeant O'Connor heartily concurred in this sentiment, reflecting how fortunate it was that Elsie was being approached unofficially. On interrogation by Sergeant O'Connor of the Police, she would have virtuously protested that she had not overheard anything at all.

'As I say,' went on Elsie, 'Dr Roberts, he was very quiet – the master was doing all the shouting.'

'What was he saying?' asked O'Connor, for the second time approaching the vital point.

'Abusing of him proper,' said Elsie with relish.

'How do you mean?'

Would the girl never come to actual words and phrases?

'Well, I don't understand a lot of it,' admitted Elsie. 'There were a lot of long words, "unprofessional conduct," and "taking advantage," and things like that – and I heard him say he'd get Dr Roberts struck off the – Medical Register, would it be? Something like that.'

'That's right,' said O'Connor. 'Complain to the Medical Council.'

'Yes, he said something like that. And the Missus was going on in sort of hysterics, saying "You never cared for me. You neglected me. You left me alone." And I heard her say that Dr Roberts had been an angel of goodness to her.

'And then the doctor, he came through into the dressing-room with the master and shut the door of the bedroom – and he said quite plain:

'"My good man, don't you realize your wife's hysterical? She doesn't know what she's saying. To tell you the truth, it's been a very difficult and trying case, and I'd have thrown it up long ago if I'd thought it was con – con – some long word; oh, yes, consistent – that was it – consistent with my duty." That's what he said. He said something about not over-stepping a boundary, too – something between doctor and patient. He got the master quietened a bit, and then he said:

'"You'll be late at the office, you know. You'd better be off. Just think things over quietly. I think you'll realize that the whole business is a mare's nest. I'll just wash my hands here before I go on to my next case. Now, you think it over, my dear fellow. I can assure you that the whole thing arises out of your wife's disordered imagination."

'And the master, he said, "I don't know what to think."

'And he come out – and, of course, I was brushing hard – but he never even noticed me. I thought afterwards he looked ill. The doctor, he was whistling quite cheerily and washing his hands in the dressing-room, where there was hot and cold laid on. And presently he came out, with his bag, and he spoke to me very nicely and cheerily, as he always did, and he went down the stairs, quite cheerful and gay and his usual self. So you see, I'm quite sure as he hadn't done anything wrong. It was all her.'

'And then Craddock got this anthrax?'

'Yes, I think he'd got it already. The mistress, she nursed him very devoted, but he died. Lovely wreaths there was at the funeral.'

'And afterwards? Did Dr Roberts come to the house again?'

'No, he didn't, Nosey! You've got some grudge against him. I tell you there was nothing in it. If there were he'd have married her when the master was dead, wouldn't he? And he never did. No such fool. He'd taken her measure all right. She used to ring him up, though, but somehow he was never in. And then she sold the house, and we all got our notices, and she went abroad to Egypt.'

'And you didn't see Dr Roberts in all that time?'

'No. *She* did, because she went to him to have this – what do you call it? – 'noculation against the typhoid fever. She came back with her arm ever so sore with it. If you ask me, he made it clear to her then that there was nothing doing. She didn't ring him up no more, and she went off very cheerful with a lovely lot of new clothes – all light colours, although it was the middle of winter, but she said it would be all sunshine and hot out there.'

'That's right,' said Sergeant O'Connor. 'It's too hot sometimes, I've heard. She died out there. You know that, I suppose?'

'No, indeed I didn't. Well, fancy that! She may have been worse than I thought, poor soul.'

She added with a sigh:

'I wonder what they did with all that lovely lot of clothes. They're blacks out there, so they couldn't wear them.'

'You'd have looked a treat in them, I expect,' said Sergeant O'Connor.

'Impudence,' said Elsie.

'Well, you won't have my impudence much longer,' said Sergeant O'Connor. 'I've got to go away on business for my firm.'

'You going for long?'

'May be going abroad,' said the Sergeant.

Elsie's face fell.

Though unacquainted with Lord Byron's famous poem, 'I never loved a dear gazelle,' etc., its sentiments were at that moment hers. She thought to herself:

'Funny how all the really attractive ones never come to anything. Oh, well, there's always Fred.'

Which is gratifying, since it shows that the sudden incursion of Sergeant O'Connor into Elsie's life did not affect it permanently. 'Fred' may even have been the gainer!

CHAPTER SEVENTEEN

The Evidence of Rhoda Dawes

Rhoda Dawes came out of Debenham's and stood meditatively upon the pavement. Indecision was written all over her face. It was an expressive face; each fleeting emotion showed itself in a quickly varying expression.

Quite plainly at this moment Rhoda's face said: 'Shall I or shan't I? I'd like to. . . . But perhaps I'd better not. . . .'

The commissionaire said, 'Taxi, Miss?' to her hopefully. Rhoda shook her head.

A stout woman carrying parcels with an eager 'shopping early for Christmas' expression on her face, cannoned into her severely, but still Rhoda stood stock-still, trying to make up her mind.

Chaotic odds and ends of thoughts flashed through her mind.

'After all, why shouldn't I? She asked me to – but perhaps it's just a thing she says to everyone. . . . She doesn't mean it to be taken seriously. . . . Well, after all, Anne didn't want me. She made it quite clear she'd rather go with Major Despard to the solicitor man alone. . . . And why shouldn't she? I mean, three *is* a crowd. . . . And it isn't really any business of mine. . . . It isn't as though I particularly *wanted* to see Major Despard. . . . He is nice, though. . . . I think he must have fallen for Anne. Men don't take a lot of trouble unless they have . . . I mean, it's never just kindness. . . .'

A messenger boy bumped into Rhoda and said, 'Beg pardon, Miss,' in a reproachful tone.

'Oh, dear,' thought Rhoda. 'I can't go on standing here all day. Just because I'm such an idiot that I can't make up my mind. . . . I think that coat and skirt's going to be awfully nice. I wonder if brown would have been more useful than green? No, I don't think so. Well, come on, shall I go or shan't I? Half-past three, it's quite a good time – I mean, it doesn't look as though I'm cadging a meal or anything. I might just go and look, anyway.'

She plunged across the road, turned to the right, and then to the left, up Harley Street, finally pausing by the block of flats always airily described by Mrs Oliver as 'all among the nursing homes.'

'Well, she can't eat me,' thought Rhoda, and plunged boldly into the building.

Mrs Oliver's flat was on the top floor. A uniformed attendant whisked her up in a lift and decanted her on a smart new mat outside a bright green door.

'This is awful,' thought Rhoda. 'Worse than dentists. I must go through with it now, though.'

Pink with embarrassment, she pushed the bell.

The door was opened by an elderly maid.

'Is – could I – is Mrs Oliver at home?' asked Rhoda.

The maid drew back, Rhoda entered, she was shown into a very untidy drawing-room. The maid said:

'What name shall I say, please?'

'Oh – eh – Miss Dawes – Miss Rhoda Dawes.'

The maid withdrew. After what seemed to Rhoda about a hundred years, but was really exactly a minute and forty-five seconds, the maid returned.

'Will you step this way, Miss?'

Pinker than ever, Rhoda followed her. Along a passage, round a corner, a door was opened. Nervously she entered into what seemed at first to her startled eyes to be an African forest!

Birds – masses of birds, parrots, macaws, birds unknown to ornithology, twined themselves in and out of what seemed to be a primeval forest. In the middle of this riot of bird and vegetable life, Rhoda perceived a battered kitchen-table with a typewriter on it, masses of typescript littered all over the floor and Mrs Oliver, her hair in wild confusion, rising from a somewhat rickety-looking chair.

'My dear, how nice to see you,' said Mrs Oliver, holding out a carbon-stained hand and trying with her other hand to smooth her hair, a quite impossible proceeding.

A paper bag, touched by her elbow, fell from the desk, and apples rolled energetically all over the floor.

'Never mind, my dear, don't bother, someone will pick them up some time.'

Rather breathless, Rhoda rose from a stooping position with five apples in her grasp.

'Oh, thank you – no, I shouldn't put them back in the bag. I think it's got a hole in it. Put them on the mantelpiece. That's right. Now, then, sit down and let's talk.'

Rhoda accepted a second battered chair and focussed her eyes on her hostess.

'I say, I'm terribly sorry. Am I interrupting, or anything?' she asked breathlessly.

'Well, you are and you aren't,' said Mrs Oliver. 'I *am* working, as you see. But that dreadful Finn of mine has got himself terribly tangled up. He did some awfully clever deduction with a dish of French beans, and now he's just detected deadly poison in the sage-and-onion stuffing of the Michaelmas goose, and I've just remembered ·that French beans are over by Michaelmas.'

Thrilled by this peep into the inner world of creative detective fiction, Rhoda said breathlessly, 'They might be tinned.'

'They might, of course,' said Mrs Oliver doubtfully. 'But it would rather spoil the point. I'm always getting tangled up in horticulture and things like that. People write to me and say I've got the wrong flowers all out together. As though it mattered – and anyway, they are all out together in a London shop.'

'Of course it doesn't matter,' said Rhoda loyally. 'Oh, Mrs Oliver, it must be marvellous to write.'

Mrs Oliver rubbed her forehead with a carbonny finger and said:

'Why?'

'Oh,' said Rhoda, a little taken aback. 'Because it must. It must be wonderful just to sit down and write off a whole book.'

'It doesn't happen exactly like that,' said Mrs Oliver. 'One actually has to *think*, you know. And thinking is always a bore. And you have to plan things. And then one gets stuck every now and then, and you feel you'll never get out of the mess – but you do! Writing's not particularly enjoyable. It's hard work like everything else.'

'It doesn't seem like work,' said Rhoda.

'Not to *you*,' said Mrs Oliver, 'because you don't have to do it! It feels very like work to me. Some days I can only keep going by repeating over and over to myself the amount of money I might get for my next serial rights. That spurs you on, you know. So does your bankbook when you see how much overdrawn you are.'

'I never imagined you actually typed your books yourself,' said Rhoda. 'I thought you'd have a secretary.'

'I did have a secretary, and I used to try and dictate to her, but she was so competent that it used to depress me. I felt she knew so much more about English and grammar and full stops and semi-colons than I did, that it gave me a kind of inferiority complex. Then I tried having a thoroughly incompetent secretary, but, of course, that didn't answer very well, either.'

'It must be so wonderful to be able to think of things,' said Rhoda.

'I can always think of things,' said Mrs Oliver happily. 'What is so tiring is writing them down. I always think I've finished, and then when I count up I find I've only written thirty thousand words instead of sixty thousand, and so then I have to throw in another murder and get the heroine kidnapped again. It's all very boring.'

Rhoda did not answer. She was staring at Mrs Oliver with the reverence felt by youth for celebrity – slightly tinged by disappointment.

'Do you like the wallpaper?' asked Mrs Oliver waving an airy hand. 'I'm frightfully fond of birds. The foliage is supposed to be tropical. It makes me feel it's a hot day, even when it's freezing. I can't do anything unless I feel very, very warm. But Sven Hjerson breaks the ice on his bath every morning!'

'I think it's all marvellous,' said Rhoda. 'And it's awfully nice of you to say I'm not interrupting you.'

'We'll have some coffee and toast,' said Mrs Oliver. 'Very black coffee and very hot toast. I can always eat that any time.'

She went to the door, opened it and shouted. Then she returned and said:

'What brings you to town – shopping?'

'Yes, I've been doing some shopping.'

'Is Miss Meredith up, too?'

'Yes, she's gone with Major Despard to a solicitor.'

'Solicitor, eh?'

Mrs Oliver's eyebrows rose inquiringly.

'Yes. You see, Major Despard told her she ought to have one. He's been awfully kind – he really has.'

'I was kind, too,' said Mrs Oliver, 'but it didn't seem to go down very well, did it? In fact, I think your friend rather resented my coming.'

'Oh, she didn't – really she didn't.' Rhoda wriggled on her chair in a paroxysm of embarrassment. 'That's really one reason why I wanted to come today – to explain. You see, I saw you had got it all wrong. She did seem very ungracious, but it wasn't that, really. I mean, it wasn't your coming. It was something you said.'

'Something I *said*?'

'Yes. You couldn't tell, of course. It was just unfortunate.'

'What did I say?'

'I don't expect you remember, even. It was just the way you put it. You said something about an accident and poison.'

'Did I?'

'I knew you'd probably not remember. Yes. You see, Anne had a ghastly experience once. She was in a house where a woman took some poison – hat paint, I think it was – by mistake for something else. And she died. And, of course, it was an awful shock to Anne. She can't bear thinking of it or speaking of it. And your saying that reminded her, of course, and she dried up and got all stiff and queer like she does. And I saw you noticed it. And I couldn't say anything in front of her. But I did want you to know that it wasn't what you thought. She wasn't ungrateful.'

Mrs Oliver looked at Rhoda's flushed eager face. She said slowly:

'I see.'

'Anne's awfully sensitive,' said Rhoda. 'And she's bad about – well, facing things. If anything's upset her, she'd just rather not talk about it, although that isn't any good, really – at least, I don't think so. Things are there just the same – whether you talk about them or not. It's only running away from them to pretend they don't exist. I'd rather have it all out, however painful it would be.'

'Ah,' said Mrs Oliver quietly. 'But you, my dear, are a soldier. Your Anne isn't.'

Rhoda flushed.

'Anne's a darling.'

Mrs Oliver smiled.

She said, 'I didn't say she wasn't. I only said she hadn't got your particular brand of courage.'

She sighed, then said rather unexpectedly to the girl:

'Do you believe in the value of truth, my dear, or don't you?'

'Of course I believe in the truth,' said Rhoda staring.

'Yes, you say that – but perhaps you haven't thought about it. The truth hurts sometimes – and destroys one's illusions.'

'I'd rather have it, all the same,' said Rhoda.

'So would I. But I don't know that we're wise.'

Rhoda said earnestly:

'Don't tell Anne, will you, what I've told you? She wouldn't like it.'

'I certainly shouldn't dream of doing any such thing. Was this long ago?

'About four years ago. It's odd, isn't it, how the same things happen again and again to people. I had an aunt who was always in shipwrecks. And here's Anne mixed up in two sudden deaths – only, of course, this one is much worse. Murder's rather awful, isn't it?'

'Yes, it is.'

The black coffee and the hot buttered toast appeared at this minute.

Rhoda ate and drank with childish gusto. It was very exciting to her thus to be sharing an intimate meal with a celebrity.

When they had finished she rose and said:

'I do hope I haven't interrupted you too terribly. Would you mind – I mean, would it bother you awfully – if I sent one of your books to you, would you sign it for me?'

'Mrs Oliver laughed.

'Oh, I can do better than that for you.' She opened a cupboard at the far end of the room. 'Which would you like? I rather fancy *The Affair of the Second Goldfish* myself. It's not quite such frightful tripe as the rest.'

A little shocked at hearing an authoress thus describe the children of her pen, Rhoda accepted eagerly. Mrs Oliver took the book, opened it, inscribed her name with a superlative flourish and handed it to Rhoda.

'There you are.'

'Thank you very much. I have enjoyed myself. Sure you didn't mind my coming?'

'I wanted you to,' said Mrs Oliver.

She added after a moment's pause:

'You're a nice child. Goodbye. Take care of yourself, my dear.'

'Now, why did I say that?' she murmured to herself as the door closed behind her guest.

She shook her head, ruffled her hair, and returned to the masterly dealings of Sven Hjerson with the sage-and-onion stuffing.

CHAPTER EIGHTEEN

Tea Interlude

Mrs Lorrimer came out of a certain door in Harley Street.

She stood for a minute at the top of the steps, and then she descended them slowly.

There was a curious expression on her face – a mingling of grim determination and of strange indecision. She bent her brows a little, as though to concentrate on some all-absorbing problem.

It was just then that she caught sight of Anne Meredith on the opposite pavement.

Anne was standing staring up at a big block of flats just on the corner.

Mrs Lorrimer hesitated a moment, then she crossed the road.

'How do you do, Miss Meredith?'

Anne started and turned.

'Oh, how do you do?'

'Still in London?' said Mrs Lorrimer.

'No. I've only come up for the day. To do some legal business.'

Her eyes were still straying to the big block of flats.

Mrs Lorrimer said:

'Is anything the matter?'

Anne started guiltily.

'The matter? Oh, no, what should be the matter?'

'You were looking as though you had something on your mind.'

'I haven't – well, at least I have, but it's nothing important, something quite silly.' She laughed a little.

She went on:

'It's only that I thought I saw my friend – the girl I live with – go in there, and I wondered if she'd gone to see Mrs Oliver.'

'Is that where Mrs Oliver lives? I didn't know.'

'Yes. She came to see us the other day and she gave us her address and asked us to come and see her. I wondered if it was Rhoda I saw or not.'

'Do you want to go up and see?'

'No, I'd rather not do that.'

'Come and have tea with me,' said Mrs Lorrimer. 'There is a shop quite near here that I know.'

'It's very kind of you,' said Anne, hesitating.

Side by side they walked down the street and turned into a side street. In a small pastry-cook's they were served with tea and muffins.

They did not talk much. Each of them seemed to find the other's silence restful.

Anne asked suddenly:

'Has Mrs Oliver been to see you?'

Mrs Lorrimer shook her head.

'No one has been to see me except M. Poirot.'

'I didn't mean –' began Anne.

'Didn't you? I think you did,' said Mrs Lorrimer.

The girl looked up – a quick, frightened glance. Something she saw in Mrs Lorrimer's face seemed to reassure her.

'He hasn't been to see me,' she said slowly.

There was a pause.

'Hasn't Superintendent Battle been to see you?' asked Anne.

'Oh, yes, of course,' said Mrs Lorrimer.

Anne said hesitatingly:

'What sort of things did he ask you?'

Mrs Lorrimer sighed wearily.

'The usual things, I suppose. Routine inquiries. He was very pleasant over it all.'

'I suppose he interviewed every one?'

'I should think so.'

There was another pause.

Anne said:

'Mrs Lorrimer, do you think – they will ever find out who did it?'

Her eyes were bent on her plate. She did not see the curious expression in the older woman's eyes as she watched the downcast head.

Mrs Lorrimer said quietly:

'I don't know. . . .'

Anne murmured:

"It's not – very nice, is it?"

There was that same curious appraising and yet sympathetic look on Mrs Lorrimer's face, as she asked:

'How old are you, Anne Meredith?'

'I – I?' the girl stammered. 'I'm twenty-five.'

'And I'm sixty-three,' said Mrs Lorrimer.

She went on slowly:

'Most of your life is in front of you. . . .'

Anne shivered.

'I might be run over by a bus on the way home,' she said.

'Yes, that's true. And I – might not.'

She said it in an odd way. Anne looked at her in astonishment.

'Life is a difficult business,' said Mrs Lorrimer. 'You'll know that when you come to my age. It needs infinite courage and a lot of endurance. And in the end one wonders: "Was it worth while?"'

'Oh, *don't*,' said Anne.

Mrs Lorrimer laughed, her old competent self again.

'It's rather cheap to say gloomy things about life,' she said.

She called the waitress and settled the bill.

As they got to the shop door a taxi crawled past, and Mrs Lorrimer hailed it.

'Can I give you a lift?' she asked. 'I am going south of the park.'

Anne's face had lighted up.

'No, thank you. I see my friend turning the corner. Thank you so much, Mrs Lorrimer. Goodbye.'

'Goodbye. Good luck,' said the older woman.

She drove away and Anne hurried forward.

Rhoda's face lit up when she saw her friend, then changed to a slightly guilty expression.

'Rhoda, have you been to see Mrs Oliver?' demanded Anne.

'Well, as a matter of fact, I have.'

'And I just caught you.'

'I don't know what you mean by caught. Let's go down here and take a bus. You'd gone off on your own ploys with the boy friend. I thought at least he'd give you tea.'

Anne was silent for a minute – a voice ringing in her ears.

'Can't we pick up your friend somewhere and all have tea together?'

And her own answer – hurried, without taking time to think:

'Thanks awfully, but we've got to go out to tea together with some people.'

A lie – and such a silly lie. The stupid way one said the first thing that came into one's head instead of just taking a minute or two to think. Perfectly easy to have said 'Thanks, but my friend has got to go out to tea.' That is, if you didn't, as she hadn't, wanted to have Rhoda too.

Rather odd, that, the way she hadn't wanted Rhoda. She had wanted, definitely, to keep Despard to herself. She had felt jealous. Jealous of Rhoda. Rhoda was so bright, so ready to talk, so full of enthusiasm and life. The other evening Major Despard had looked as though he thought Rhoda nice. But it was her, Anne Meredith, he had come down to see. Rhoda was like that. She didn't mean it, but she reduced you to the background. No, definitely she hadn't wanted Rhoda there.

But she had managed it very stupidly, getting flurried like that. If she'd managed better, she might be sitting now having tea with Major Despard at his club or somewhere.

She felt definitely annoyed with Rhoda. Rhoda was a nuisance. And what had she been doing going to see Mrs Oliver?

Out loud she said:

'Why did you go and see Mrs Oliver?'

'Well, she asked us to.'

'Yes, but I didn't suppose she really meant it. I expect she always has to say that.'

'She did mean it. She was awfully nice – couldn't have been nicer. She gave me one of her books. Look.'

Rhoda flourished her prize.

Anne said suspiciously:

'What did you talk about? Not me?'

'Listen to the conceit of the girl!'

'No, but did you? Did you talk about the – the murder?'

'We talked about her murders. She's writing one where there's poison in the sage and onions. She was frightfully human – and said writing was awfully hard work and how she got into tangles with plots, and we had black coffee and hot buttered toast,' finished Rhoda in a triumphant burst.

Then she added:

'Oh, Anne, you want your tea.'

'No, I don't. I've had it. With Mrs Lorrimer.'

'Mrs Lorrimer? Isn't that the one – the one who was there?'

Anne nodded.

'Where did you come across her? Did you go and see her?'

'No. I ran across her in Harley Street.'

'What was she like?'

Anne said slowly:

'I don't know. She was – rather queer. Not at all like the other night.'

'Do you still think she did it?' asked Rhoda.

Anne was silent for a minute or two. Then she said:

'I don't know. Don't let's talk of it, Rhoda! You know how I hate talking of things.'

'All right, darling. What was the solicitor like? Very dry and legal?'

'Rather alert and Jewish.'

'Sounds all right.' She waited a little and then said:

'How was Major Despard?'

'Very kind.'

'He's fallen for you, Anne. I'm sure he has.'

'Rhoda, don't talk nonsense.'

'Well, you'll see.'

Rhoda began humming to herself. She thought:

'Of course he's fallen for her. Anne's awfully pretty. But a bit wishy-washy. . . . She'll never go on treks with him. Why, she'd scream if she saw a snake. . . . Men always do take fancies to unsuitable women.'

Then she said aloud.

'That bus will take us to Paddington. We'll just catch the 4.48.'

CHAPTER NINETEEN

Consultation

The telephone rang in Poirot's room and a respectful voice spoke.

'Sergeant O'Connor. Superintendent Battle's compliments and would it be convenient for Mr Hercule Poirot to come to Scotland Yard at 11.30?'

Poirot replied in the affirmative and Sergeant O'Connor rang off.

It was 11.30 to the minute when Poirot descended from his taxi at the door of New Scotland Yard – to be at once seized upon by Mrs Oliver.

'M. Poirot. How splendid! Will you come to my rescue?'

'*Enchanté*, madame. What can I do?'

'Pay my taxi for me. I don't know how it happened but I brought out the bag I keep my going-abroad money in and the man simply won't take francs or liras or marks!'

Poirot gallantly produced some loose change, and he and Mrs Oliver went inside the building together.

They were taken to Superintendent Battle's own room. The superintendent was sitting behind a table and looking more wooden than ever. 'Just like a little piece of modern sculpture,' whispered Mrs Oliver to Poirot.

Battle rose and shook hands with them both and they sat down.

'I thought it was about time for a little meeting,' said Battle. 'You'd like to hear how I've got on, and I'd like to hear how you've got on. We're just waiting for Colonel Race and then –'

But at that moment the door opened and the colonel appeared.

'Sorry I'm late, Battle. How do you do, Mrs Oliver.

Hallo, M. Poirot. Very sorry if I've kept you waiting. But I'm off tomorrow and had a lot of things to see to.'

'Where are you going to?' asked Mrs Oliver.

'A little shooting trip – Baluchistan way.'

Poirot said, smiling ironically:

'A little trouble, is there not, in that part of the world? You will have to be careful.'

'I mean to be,' said Race gravely – but his eyes twinkled.

'Got anything for us, sir?' asked Battle.

'I've got you your information re Despard. Here it is –'

He pushed over a sheaf of papers.

'There's a mass of dates and places there. Most of it quite irrelevant, I should imagine. Nothing against him. He's a stout fellow. Record quite unblemished. Strict disciplinarian. Liked and trusted by the natives everywhere. One of their cumbrous names for him in Africa, where they go in for such things, is "The man who keeps his mouth shut and judges fairly." General opinion of the white races that Despard is a Pukka Sahib. Fine shot. Cool head. Generally long-sighted and dependable.'

Unmoved by this eulogy, Battle asked:

'Any sudden deaths connected with him?'

'I laid special stress on that point. There's one fine rescue to his credit. Pal of his was being mauled by a lion.'

Battle sighed.

'It's not rescues I want.'

'You're a persistent fellow, Battle. There's only one incident I've been able to rake up that might suit your book. Trip into the interior in South America. Despard accompanied Professor Luxmore, the celebrated botanist, and his wife. The professor died of fever and was buried somewhere up the Amazon.'

'Fever – eh?'

'Fever. But I'll play fair with you. One of the native bearers (who was sacked for stealing, incidentally) had a story that the professor didn't die of fever, but was shot. The rumour was never taken seriously.'

'About time it was, perhaps.'

Race shook his head.

'I've given you the facts. You asked for them and you're entitled to them, but I'd lay long odds against its being Despard who did the dirty work the other evening. He's a white man, Battle.'

'Incapable of murder, you mean?'

Colonel Race hesitated.

'Incapable of what I'd call murder – yes,' he said.

'But not incapable of killing a man for what would seem to him good and sufficient reasons, is that it?'

'If so, they *would* be good and sufficient reasons!'

Battle shook his head.

'You can't have human beings judging other human beings and taking the law into their own hands.'

'It happens, Battle – it happens.'

'It shouldn't happen – that's my point. What do you say, M. Poirot?'

'I agree with you, Battle. I have always disapproved of murder.'

'What a delightfully droll way of putting it,' said Mrs Oliver. 'Rather as though it were fox-hunting or killing ospreys for hats. Don't you think there are people who ought to be murdered?'

'That, very possibly.'

'Well then!'

'You do not comprehend. It is not the victim who concerns me so much. It is the effect on the character of the slayer.'

'What about war?'

'In war you do not exercise the right of private judgement. *That* is what is so dangerous. Once a man is imbued with the idea that he knows who ought to be allowed to live and who ought not – then he is halfway to

144

becoming the most dangerous killer there is – the arrogant criminal who kills not for profit – but for an idea. He has usurped the functions of *le bon Dieu*.'

Colonel Race rose:

'I'm sorry I can't stop with you. Too much to do. I'd like to see the end of this business. Shouldn't be surprised if there never was an end. Even if you find out who did it, it's going to be next to impossible to prove. I've given you the facts you wanted, but in my opinion Despard's not the man. I don't believe he's ever committed murder. Shaitana may have heard some garbled rumour of Professor Luxmore's death, but I don't believe there's more to it than that. Despard's a white man, and I don't believe he's ever been a murderer. That's my opinion. And I know something of men.'

'What's Mrs Luxmore like?' asked Battle.

'She lives in London, so you can see for yourself. You'll find the address among those papers. Somewhere in South Kensington. But I repeat, Despard isn't the man.'

Colonel Race left the room, stepping with the springy noiseless tread of a hunter.

Battle nodded his head thoughtfully as the door closed behind him.

'He's probably right,' he said. 'He knows men, Colonel Race does. But all the same, one can't take anything for granted.'

He looked through the mass of documents Race had deposited on the table, occasionally making a pencil note on the pad beside him.

'Well, Superintendent Battle,' said Mrs Oliver. 'Aren't you going to tell us what you have been doing?'

He looked up and smiled, a slow smile that creased his wooden face from side to side.

'This is all very irregular, Mrs Oliver. I hope you realize that.'

'Nonsense,' said Mrs Oliver. 'I don't suppose for a moment you'll tell us anything you don't want to.'

Battle shook his head.

'No,' he said decidedly. 'Cards on the table. That's the motto for this business. I mean to play fair.'

Mrs Oliver hitched her chair nearer.

'Tell us,' she begged.

Superintendent Battle said slowly:

'First of all, I'll say this. As far as the actual murder of Mr Shaitana goes, I'm not a penny the wiser. There's no hint or clue of any kind to be found in his papers. As for the four others, I've had them shadowed, naturally, but without any tangible result. No, as M. Poirot said, there's only one hope – the past. Find out what crime exactly (if any, that is to say – after all, Shaitana may have been talking through his hat to make an impression on M. Poirot) these people have committed – and it may tell you who committed this crime.'

'Well, have you found out anything?'

'I've got a line on one of them.'

'Which?'

'Dr Roberts.'

Mrs Oliver looked at him with thrilled expectation.

'As M. Poirot here knows, I tried out all kinds of theories. I established the fact pretty clearly that none of his immediate family had met with a sudden death. I've explored every alley as well as I could, and the whole thing boils down to one possibility – and rather an outside possibility at that. A few years ago Roberts must have been guilty of indiscretion, at least, with one of his lady patients. There may have been nothing in it – probably wasn't. But the woman was the hysterical, emotional kind who likes to make a scene, and either the husband got wind of what was going on, or his wife "confessed". Anyway, the fat was in the fire as far as the doctor was concerned. Enraged husband threatening to report him to the General Medical Council – which would probably have meant the ruin of his professional career.'

'What happened?' demanded Mrs Oliver breathlessly.

'Apparently Roberts managed to calm down the irate gentleman temporarily – and he died of anthrax almost immediately afterwards.'

'Anthtrax? But that's a cattle disease?'

The superintendent grinned.

'Quite right, Mrs Oliver. It isn't the untraceable arrow poison of the South American Indians! You may remember that there was rather a scare about infected shaving brushes of cheap make about that time. Craddock's shaving brush was proved to have been the cause of infection.'

'Did Dr Roberts attend him?'

'Oh, no. Too canny for that. Dare say Craddock wouldn't have wanted him in any case. The only evidence I've got – and that's precious little – is that among the doctor's patients there *was* a case of anthrax at the time.'

'You mean the doctor infected the shaving brush?'

'That's the big idea. And mind you, it's only an idea. Nothing whatever to go on. Pure conjecture. But it could be.'

'He didn't marry Mrs Craddock afterwards?'

'Oh, dear me, no, I imagine the affection was always on the lady's side. She tended to cut up rough, I hear, but suddenly went off to Egypt quite happily for the winter. She died there. A case of some obscure blood-poisoning. It's got a long name, but I don't expect it would convey much to you. Most uncommon in this country, fairly common among the natives in Egypt.'

'So the doctor couldn't have poisoned her?'

'I don't know,' said Battle slowly. 'I've been chatting to a bacteriologist friend of mine – awfully difficult to get straight answers out of these people. They never can say yes or no. It's always "that might be possible under certain conditions" – "it would depend on the pathological condition of the recipient" – "such cases have been known" – "a lot depends on individual idiosyncrasy" – all that sort of stuff. But as far as I could pin my friend down I got at this –

the germ, or germs, I suppose, might have been introduced into the blood before leaving England. The symptoms would not make their appearance for some time to come.'

Poirot asked:

'Was Mrs Craddock inoculated for typhoid before going to Egypt? Most people are, I fancy.'

'Good for you, M. Poirot.'

'And Dr Roberts did the inoculation?'

'That's right. There you are again – we can't prove anything. She had the usual two inoculations – and they may have been typhoid inoculations for all we know. Or one of them may have been typhoid inoculation and the other – something else. We don't know. We never shall know. The whole thing is pure hypothesis. All we can say is: it might be.'

Poirot nodded thoughtfully.

'It agrees very well with some remarks made to me by Mr Shaitana. He was exalting the successful murderer – the man against whom his crime could never be brought home.'

'How did Mr Shaitana know about it, then?' asked Mrs Oliver.

Poirot shrugged his shoulders.

'That we shall never learn. He himself was in Egypt at one time. We know that, because he met Mrs Lorrimer there. He may have heard some local doctor comment on curious features of Mrs Craddock's case – a wonder as to how the infection arose. At some other time he may have heard gossip about Roberts and Mrs Craddock. He might have amused himself by making some cryptic remark to the doctor and noted the startled awareness in his eye – all that one can never know. Some people have an uncanny gift of divining secrets. Mr Shaitana was one of those people. All that does not concern us. We have only to say – he guessed. Did he guess right?'

'Well, I think he did,' said Battle. 'I've a feeling that our cheerful, genial doctor wouldn't be too scrupulous. I've known one or two like him – wonderful how certain types resemble each other. In my opinion he's a killer all right. He killed Craddock. He may have killed Mrs Craddock if she was beginning to be a nuisance and cause a scandal. *But did he kill Shaitana?* That's the real question. And comparing the crimes, I rather doubt it. In the case of the Craddocks he used medical methods each time. The deaths appeared to be due to natural causes. In my opinion if he had killed Shaitana, he would have done so in a medical way. He'd have used the germ and not the knife.'

'I never thought it was him,' said Mrs Oliver. 'Not for a minute. He's too obvious, somehow.'

'Exit Roberts,' murmured Poirot. 'And the others?'

Battle made a gesture of impatience.

'I've pretty well drawn blank. Mrs Lorrimer's been a widow for twenty years now. She's lived in London most of the time, occasionally going abroad in the winter. Civilized places – the Riviera, Egypt, that sort of thing. Can't find any mysterious death associated with her. She seems to have led a perfectly normal, respectable life – the life of a woman of the world. Everyone seems to respect her and to have the highest opinion of her character. The worst that they can say about her is that she doesn't suffer fools gladly! I don't mind admitting I've been beaten all along the line there. And yet there must be *something*! Shaitana thought there was.'

He sighed in a dispirited manner.

'Then there's Miss Meredith. I've got her history taped out quite clearly. Usual sort of story. Army officer's daughter. Left with very little money. Had to earn her living. Not properly trained for anything. I've checked up on her early days at Cheltenham. All quite straightforward. Everyone very sorry for the poor little thing. She went first to some people in the Isle of Wight – kind of nursery-governess and mother's help. The woman she was with is out in Palestine but I've talked with her sister and she says

Mrs Eldon liked the girl very much. Certainly no mysterious deaths nor anything of that kind.

'When Mrs Eldon went abroad, Miss Meredith went to Devonshire and took a post as companion to an aunt of a school friend. The school friend is the girl she is living with now – Miss Rhoda Dawes. She was there over two years until Miss Dawes got too ill and she had to have a regular trained nurse. Cancer, I gather. She's alive still, but very vague. Kept under morphia a good deal, I imagine. I had an interview with her. She remembered "Anne," said she was a nice child. I also talked to a neighbour of hers who would be better able to remember the happenings of the last few years. No deaths in the parish except one or two of the older villagers, with whom, as far as I can make out, Anne Meredith never came into contact.

'Since then there's been Switzerland. Thought I might get on the track of some fatal accident there, but nothing doing. And there's nothing in Wallingford either.'

'So Anne Meredith is acquitted?' asked Poirot.

Battle hesitated.

'I wouldn't say that. There's *something*. . . . There's a scared look about her that can't quite be accounted for by panic over Shaitana. She's too watchful. Too much on the alert. I'd swear there was *something*. But there it is – she's led a perfectly blameless life.'

Mrs Oliver took a deep breath – a breath of pure enjoyment.

'And yet,' she said, 'Anne Meredith was in the house when a woman took poison by mistake and died.'

She had nothing to complain of in the effect her words produced.

Superintendent Battle spun round in his chair and stared at her in amazement.

'Is this true, Mrs Oliver? How do you know?'

'I've been sleuthing,' said Mrs Oliver. 'I get on with girls. I went down to see those two and told them a cock-and-bull story about suspecting Dr Roberts. The Rhoda girl was friendly – oh, and rather impressed by thinking I was a celebrity. The little Meredith hated my coming and showed it quite plainly. She was suspicious. Why should she be if she hadn't got anything to hide? I asked either of them to come and see me in London. The Rhoda girl did. And she blurted the whole thing out. How Anne had been rude to me the other day because something I'd said had reminded her of a painful incident, and then she went on to describe the incident.'

'Did she say when and where it happened?'

'Three years ago in Devonshire.'

The superintendent muttered something under his breath and scribbled on his pad. His wooden calm was shaken.

Mrs Oliver sat enjoying her triumph. It was a moment of great sweetness to her.

'I take off my hat to you, Mrs Oliver,' he said. 'You've put one over on us this time. That is very valuable information. And it just shows how easily you can miss a thing.'

He frowned a little.

'She can't have been there – wherever it was – long. A couple of months at most. It must have been between the Isle of Wight and going to Miss Dawes. Yes, that could be it right enough. Naturally Mrs Eldon's sister only remembers she went off to a place in Devonshire – she doesn't remember exactly who or where.'

'Tell me,' said Poirot, 'was this Mrs Eldon an untidy woman?'

Battle bent a curious gaze upon him.

'It's odd your saying that, M. Poirot. I don't see how you could have known. The sister was rather a precise party. In talking I remember her saying "My sister is so dreadfully untidy and slapdash." But how did *you* know?'

'Because she needed a mother's-help,' said Mrs Oliver.

Poirot shook his head.

'No, no, it was not that. It is of no moment. I was only curious. Continue, Superintendent Battle.'

'In the same way,' went on Battle, 'I took it for granted that she went to Miss Dawes straight from the Isle of Wight. She's sly, that girl. She deceived me all right. Lying the whole time.'

'Lying is not always a sign of guilt,' said Poirot.

'I know that, M. Poirot. There's the natural liar. I should say she was one, as a matter of fact. Always says the thing that sounds best. But all the same it's a pretty grave risk to take, suppressing facts like that.'

'She wouldn't know you had any idea of past crimes,' said Mrs Oliver.

'That's all the more reason for not suppressing that little piece of information. It must have been accepted as a bona fide case of accidental death, so she'd nothing to fear – *unless she were guilty.*'

'Unless she were guilty of the Devonshire death, yes,' said Poirot.

Battle turned to him.

'Oh, I know. Even if that accidental death turns out to be not so accidental, *it doesn't follow that she killed Shaitana.* But these other murders are murders too. I want to be able to bring home a crime to the person responsible for it.'

'According to Mr Shaitana, that is impossible,' remarked Poirot.

'It is in Roberts' case. It remains to be seen if it is in Miss Meredith's. I shall go down to Devon tomorrow.'

'Will you know where to go?' asked Mrs Oliver. 'I didn't like to ask Rhoda for more details.'

'No, that was wise of you. I shan't have much difficulty. There must have been an inquest. I shall find it in the coroner's records. That's routine police work. They'll have it all taped out for me by tomorrow morning.'

'What about Major Despard?' asked Mrs Oliver. 'Have you found out anything about him?'

'I've been waiting for Colonel Race's report. I've had him shadowed, of course. One rather interesting thing, he went down to see Miss Meredith at Wallingford. You remember he said he'd never met her until the other night.'

'But she is a very pretty girl,' murmured Poirot.

Battle laughed.

'Yes, I expect that's all there is to it. By the way, Despard's taking no chances. He's already consulted a solicitor. That looks as though he's expecting trouble.'

'He is a man who looks ahead,' said Poirot. 'He is a man who prepares for every contingency.'

'And therefore not the kind of man to stick a knife into a man in a hurry,' said Battle with a sigh.

'Not unless it was the only way,' said Poirot. 'He can act quickly, remember.'

Battle looked across the table at him.

'Now, M. Poirot, what about your cards? Haven't seen your hand down on the table yet.'

Poirot smiled.

'There is so little in it. You think I conceal facts from you? It is not so. I have not learned many facts. I have talked with Dr Roberts, with Mrs Lorrimer, with Major Despard (I have still to talk to Miss Meredith) and what have I learnt? This! That Dr Roberts is a keen observer, that Mrs Lorrimer on the other hand has a most remarkable power of concentration but is, in consequence, almost blind to her surroundings. But she is fond of flowers. Despard notices only those things which appeal to him – rugs, trophies of sport. He has neither what I call the outward vision (seeing details all around you – what is called an observant person) nor the inner vision – concentration, the focusing of the mind on one object. He has a purposefully limited vision. He sees only what blends and harmonizes with the bent of his mind.'

'So those are what you call facts – eh?' said Battle curiously.

'They *are* facts – very small fry – perhaps.'

'What about Miss Meredith?'

'I have left her to the end. But I shall question her too as to what she remembers in that room.'

'It's an odd method of approach,' said Battle thoughtfully. 'Purely psychological. Suppose they're leading you up the garden path?'

Poirot shook his head with a smile.

'No, that would be impossible. Whether they try to hinder or to help, they necessarily reveal their *type of mind*.'

'There's something in it, no doubt, said Battle thoughtfully. 'I couldn't work that way myself, though.'

Poirot said, still smiling:

'I feel I have done very little in comparison with you and with Mrs Oliver – and with Colonel Race. My cards, that I place on the table, are very low ones.'

Battle twinkled at him.

'As to that, M. Poirot, the two of trumps is a low card but it can take any one of three aces. All the same, I'm going to ask you to do a practical job of work.'

'And that is?'

'I want you to interview Professor Luxmore's widow.'

'Why do you not do that yourself?'

'Because, as I said just now, I'm off to Devonshire.'

'Why do you not do that yourself?' repeated Poirot.

'Won't be put off, will you? Well, I'll speak the truth. I think you'll get more out of her than I shall.'

'My methods being less straightforward?'

'You can put it that way if you like,' said Battle grinning. 'I've heard Inspector Japp say that you've got a tortuous mind.'

'Like the late Mr Shaitana?'

'You think he would have been able to get things out of her?'

Poirot said slowly:

'I rather think he *did* get things out of her!'

154

'What makes you think so?' asked Battle sharply.

'A chance remark of Major Despard's.'

'Gave himself away, did he? That sounds unlike him.'

'Oh, my dear friend, it is impossible *not* to give oneself away – unless one never opens one's mouth! Speech is the deadliest of revealers.'

'Even if people tell lies?' asked Mrs Oliver.

'Yes, madame, because it can be seen at once that you tell *a certain kind of lie*.'

'You make me feel quite uncomfortable,' said Mrs Oliver, getting up.

Superintendent Battle accompanied her to the door and shook her by the hand.

'You've been the goods, Mrs Oliver,' he said. 'You're a much better detective than that long lanky Laplander of yours.'

'Finn,' corrected Mrs Oliver. 'Of course he's idiotic. But people like him. Goodbye.'

'I, too, must depart,' said Poirot.

Battle scribbled an address on a piece of paper and shoved it into Poirot's hand.

'There you are. Go and tackle her.'

Poirot smiled.

'And what do you want me to find out?'

'The truth about Professor Luxmore's death.'

'*Mon cher* Battle! Does anybody know the truth about anything?'

'I'm going to about this business in Devonshire,' said the superintendent with decision.

Poirot murmured:

'I wonder.'

CHAPTER TWENTY

The Evidence of Mrs Luxmore

The maid who opened the door at Mrs Luxmore's South Kensington address looked at Hercule Poirot with deep disapproval. She showed no disposition to admit him into the house.

Unperturbed, Poirot gave her a card.

'Give that to your mistress. I think she will see me.'

It was one of his more ostentatious cards. The words 'Private Detective' were printed in one corner. He had had them specially engraved for the purpose of obtaining interviews with the so-called fair sex. Nearly every woman, whether conscious of innocence or not, was anxious to have a look at a private detective and find out what he wanted.

Left ignominiously on the mat, Poirot studied the doorknocker with intense disgust at its unpolished condition.

'Ah! for some Brasso and a rag,' he murmured to himself.

Breathing excitedly the maid returned and Poirot was bidden to enter.

He was shown into a room on the first floor – a rather dark room smelling of stale flowers and unemptied ashtrays. There were large quantities of silk cushions of exotic colours all in need of cleaning. The walls were emerald green and the ceiling was of pseudo copper.

A tall, rather handsome woman was standing by the mantelpiece. She came forward and spoke in a deep husky voice.

'M. Hercule Poirot?'

Poirot bowed. His manner was not quite his own. He was not only foreign but ornately foreign. His gestures were positively baroque. Faintly, very faintly, it was the manner of the late Mr Shaitana.

'What did you want to see me about?'

Again Poirot bowed.

'If I might be seated? It will take a little time –'

She waved him impatiently to a chair and sat down herself on the edge of a sofa.

'Yes? Well?'

'It is, madame, that I make the inquiries – the private inquiries, you understand?'

The more deliberate his approach, the greater her eagerness.

'Yes – yes?'

'I make inquiries into the death of the late Professor Luxmore.'

She gave a gasp. Her dismay was evident.

'But why? What do you mean? What has it got to do with you?'

Poirot watched her carefully before proceeding.

'There is, you comprehend, a book being written. A life of your eminent husband. The writer, naturally, is anxious to get all his facts exact. As to your husband's death, for instance –'

She broke in at once:

'My husband died of fever – on the Amazon.'

Poirot leaned back in his chair. Slowly, very, very slowly, he shook his head to and fro – a maddening, monotonous motion.

'Madame – madame – ' he protested.

'But I know! I was there at the time.'

'Ah, yes, certainly. You were *there*. Yes, my information says so.'

She cried out:

'What information?'

Eyeing her closely Poirot said:

'Information supplied to me by the late Mr Shaitana.'

She shrank back as though flicked with a whip.

'Shaitana?' she muttered.

'A man,' said Poirot, 'possessed of vast stores of knowledge. A remarkable man. That man knew many secrets.'

'I suppose he did,' she murmured, passing a tongue over her dry lips.

Poirot leaned forward. He achieved a little tap on her knee.

'He knew, for instance, that your husband did not die of fever.'

She stared at him. Her eyes looked wild and desperate.

He leaned back and watched the effect of his words.

She pulled herself together with an effort.

'I don't – I don't know what you mean.'

It was very unconvincingly said.

'Madame,' said Poirot, 'I will come out into the open. I will,' he smiled, 'place my cards upon the table. Your husband did not die of fever. *He died of a bullet!*'

'Oh!' she cried.

She covered her face with her hands. She rocked herself to and fro. She was in terrible distress. But somewhere, in some remote fibre of her being, she was enjoying her own emotions. Poirot was quite sure of that.

'And therefore,' said Poirot in a matter-of-fact tone, 'you might just as well tell me the whole story.'

She uncovered her face and said:

'It wasn't in the least way you think.'

Again Poirot leaned forward – again he tapped her knee.

'You misunderstand me – you misunderstand me utterly,' he said. 'I know very well that it was not you who shot him. It was Major Despard. But you were the cause.'

'I don't know. I don't know. I suppose I was. It was all too terrible. There is a sort of fatality that pursues me.'

'Ah, how true that is,' cried Poirot. 'How often have I not seen it? There are some women like that. Wherever they go, tragedies follow in their wake. It is not their fault. These things happen in spite of themselves.'

Mrs Luxmore drew a deep breath.

'You understand. I see you understand. It all happened so naturally.'

'You travelled together into the interior, did you not?'

'Yes. My husband was writing a book on various rare plants. Major Despard was introduced to us as a man who knew the conditions and would arrange the necessary expedition. My husband liked him very much. We started.'

There was a pause. Poirot allowed it to continue for about a minute and a half and then murmured as though to himself.

'Yes, one can picture it. The winding river – the tropical night – the hum of the insects – the strong soldierly man – the beautiful woman . . .'

Mrs Luxmore sighed.

'My husband was, of course, years older than I was. I married as a mere child before I knew what I was doing . . .'

Poirot shook his head sadly.

'I know. I know. How often does that not occur?'

'Neither of us would admit what was happening,' went on Mrs Luxmore. 'John Despard never said anything. He was the soul of honour.'

'But a woman always knows,' prompted Poirot.

'How right you are . . . Yes, a woman knows . . . But I never showed him that I knew. We were Major Despard and Mrs Luxmore to each other right up to the end . . . We were both determined to play the game.'

She was silent, lost in admiration of that noble attitude.

'True,' murmured Poirot. 'One must play the cricket. As one of your poets so finely says, "I could not love thee, dear, so much, loved I not cricket more."'

'Honour,' corrected Mrs Luxmore with a slight frown.

'Of course – of course – honour. "Loved I not honour more."'

'Those words might have been written for us,'

159

murmured Mrs Luxmore. 'No matter what it cost us, we were both determined never to say the fatal word. And then –'

'And then –' prompted Poirot.

'That ghastly night.' Mrs Luxmore shuddered.

'Yes?'

'I suppose they must have quarrelled – John and Timothy, I mean. I came out of my tent. . . . I came out of my tent . . .'

'Yes – yes?'

Mrs Luxmore's eyes were wide and dark. She was seeing the scene as though it were being repeated in front of her.

'I came out of my tent,' she repeated. 'John and Timothy were – Oh!' she shuddered. 'I can't remember it all clearly. I came between them . . . I said "No – no, it isn't *true!*" Timothy wouldn't listen. He was threatening John. John had to fire – in self-defence. Ah!' she gave a cry and covered her face with her hands. 'He was dead – stone dead – shot through the heart.'

'A terrible moment for you, madame.'

'I shall never forget it. John was noble. He was all for giving himself up. I refused to hear of it. We argued all night. "For my sake," I kept saying. He saw that in the end. Naturally he couldn't let me suffer. The awful publicity. Think of the headlines. *Two Men and a Woman in the Jungle. Primeval Passions.*

'I put it all to John. In the end he gave in. The boys had seen and heard nothing. Timothy had been having a bout of fever. We said he had died of it. We buried him there beside the Amazon.'

A deep, tortured sigh shook her form.

'And then – back to civilization – and to part for ever.'

'Was it necessary, madame?'

'Yes, yes. Timothy dead stood between us just as Timothy alive had done – more so. We said goodbye to each other – for ever. I meet John Despard sometimes – out in the world. We smile, we speak politely – no one would ever guess that there was anything between us. But I see in his eyes – and he in mine – that we will never forget . . .'

There was a long pause. Poirot paid tribute to the curtain by not breaking the silence.

Mrs Luxmore took out a vanity case and powdered her nose – the spell was broken.

'What a tragedy,' said Poirot, but in a more everyday tone.

'You can see, M. Poirot,' said Mrs Luxmore earnestly, 'that the truth must never be told.'

'It would be painful –'

'It would be impossible. This friend, this writer – surely he would not wish to blight the life of a perfectly innocent woman?'

'Or even to hang a perfectly innocent man?' murmured Poirot.

'You see it like that? I am glad. He *was* innocent. A *crime passionnel* is not really a crime. And in any case it was self-defence. He *had* to shoot. So you do understand, M. Poirot, that the world must continue to think Timothy died of fever?'

Poirot murmured.

'Writers are sometimes curiously callous.'

'Your friend is a woman-hater? He wants to make us suffer? But you must not allow that. I shall not allow it. If necessary I shall take the blame on myself. I shall say *I* shot Timothy.

She had risen to her feet. Her head was thrown back.

Poirot also rose.

'Madame,' he said as he took her hand, 'such splendid self-sacrifice is unnecessary. I will do my best so that the true facts shall never be known.'

A sweet womanly smile stole over Mrs Luxmore's face. She raised her hand slightly, so that Poirot, whether he had meant to do so or not, was forced to kiss it.

'An unhappy woman thanks you, M. Poirot,' she said.

It was the last word of a persecuted queen to a favoured courtier – clearly an exit line. Poirot duly made his exit.

Once out in the street, he drew a long breath of fresh air.

CHAPTER TWENTY-ONE

Major Despard

'*Quelle femme,*' murmured Hercule Poirot. '*Ce pauvre Despard! Ce qu'il a dû souffrir! Quel voyage épouvantable!*'

Suddenly he began to laugh.

He was now walking along the Brompton Road. He paused, took out his watch, and made a calculation.

'But yes, I have the time. In any case to wait will do him no harm. I can now attend to the other little matter. What was it that my friend in the English police force used to sing – how many years – forty years ago? "A little piece of sugar for the bird."'

Humming a long-forgotten tune, Hercule Poirot entered a sumptuous-looking shop mainly devoted to the clothing and general embellishment of women and made his way to the stocking counter.

Selecting a sympathetic-looking and not too haughty damsel he made known his requirements.

'Silk stockings? Oh, yes, we have a very nice line here. Guaranteed pure silk.'

Poirot waved them away. He waxed eloquent once more.

'French silk stockings? With the duty, you know, they are very expensive.'

A fresh lot of boxes was produced.

'Very nice, mademoiselle, but I had something of a finer texture in mind.'

'These are a hundred gauge. Of course, we have some extra fine, but I'm afraid they come out at about thirty-five shillings a pair. And no durability, of course. Just like cobwebs.'

'*C'est ça. C'est ça, exactement.*'

A prolonged absence of the young lady this time.

She returned at last.

'I'm afraid they are actually thirty-seven and sixpence a pair. But beautiful, aren't they?'

She slid them tenderly from a gauzy envelope – the finest, gauziest wisps of stockings.

'*Enfin* – that is it exactly!'

'Lovely, aren't they? How many pairs, sir?'

'I want – let me see, nineteen pairs.'

The young lady very nearly fell down behind the counter, but long training in scornfulness just kept her erect.

'There would be a reduction on two dozen,' she said faintly.

'No, I want nineteen pairs. Of slightly different colours, please.'

The girl sorted them out obediently, packed them up and made out the bill.

As Poirot departed with his purchase, the next girl at the counter said:

'Wonder who the lucky girl is? Must be a nasty old man. Oh, well, she seems to be stringing him along good and proper. Stockings at thirty-seven and sixpence indeed!'

Unaware of the low estimate formed by the young ladies of Messrs Harvey Robinson's upon his character, Poirot was trotting homewards.

He had been in for about half an hour when he heard the door-bell ring. A few minutes later Major Despard entered the room.

He was obviously keeping his temper with difficulty.

'What the devil did you want to go and see Mrs Luxmore for?' he asked.

Poirot smiled.

'I wished, you see, for the true story of Professor Luxmore's death.'

'True story? Do you think that woman's capable of telling the truth about anything?' demanded Despard wrathfully.

'*Eh bien*, I did wonder now and then,' admitted Poirot.

'I should think you did. That woman's crazy.'

Poirot demurred.

'Not at all. She is a romantic woman, that is all.'

'Romantic be damned. She's an out-and-out liar. I some-times think she even believes her own lies.'

'It is quite possible.'

'She's an appalling woman. I had the hell of a time with her out there.'

'That also I can well believe.'

Despard sat down abruptly.

'Look here, M. Poirot, I'm going to tell you the truth.'

'You mean you are going to give me your version of the story?'

'My version will be the true version.'

Poirot did not reply.

Despard went on drily:

'I quite realize that I can't claim any merit in coming out with this now. I'm telling the truth because it's the only thing to be done at this stage. Whether you believe me or not is up to you. I've no kind of proof that my story is the correct one.'

He paused for a minute and then began.

'I arranged the trip for the Luxmores. He was a nice old boy quite batty about mosses and plants and things. She was a – well, she was what you've no doubt observed her to be! That trip was a nightmare. I didn't care a damn for the woman – rather disliked her, as a matter of fact. She was the intense, soulful kind that always makes me feel prickly with embarrassment. Everything went all right for the first fort-night. Then we all had a go of fever. She and I had it slightly. Old Luxmore was pretty bad. One night – now you've got to listen to this carefully – I was sitting outside my tent. Suddenly I saw Luxmore in the distance staggering off into the bush by the river. He was absolutely delirious and quite unconscious of what he was doing. In another minute he would be in the river – and at that particular spot it would have been the end of him. No chance of a rescue. There wasn't time to rush after him – only one thing to be done. My rifle was beside me as usual. I snatched it up. I'm a pretty accurate shot. I was quite sure I could bring the old boy down – get him in the leg. And then, just as I fired, that idiotic fool of a woman flung herself from somewhere upon me, yelping out, "Don't shoot. For God's sake, don't shoot." She caught my arm and jerked it ever so slightly just as the rifle went off – with the result that the bullet got him in the back and killed him dead!

'I can tell you that was a pretty ghastly moment. And that damned fool of a woman still didn't understand what she'd done. Instead of realizing that she'd been responsible for her husband's death, she firmly believed that I'd been trying to shoot the old boy in cold blood – for the love of her, if you please! We had the devil of a scene – she insisting that we should say he died of fever. I was sorry for her – especially as I saw she didn't realize what she'd done. But she'd have to realize it if the truth came out! And then her complete certainty that I was head over heels in love with her gave me a bit of a jar. It was going to be a pretty kettle of fish if she went about giving that out. In the end I agreed to do what she wanted – partly for the sake of peace, I'll admit. After all, it didn't seem to matter much. Fever or accident. And I didn't want to drag a woman through a lot of unpleasantness – even if she was a damned fool. I gave it out next day that the professor was dead of fever and we buried him. The bearers knew the truth, of course, but they were all devoted to me and I knew that what I said they'd swear to if need be. We buried poor old Luxmore and got back to civilization. Since then I've spent a good deal of time dodging the woman.'

He paused, then said quietly:

'That's my story, M. Poirot.'

Poirot said slowly:

'It was to that incident that Mr Shaitana referred, or so you thought, at dinner that night?'

Despard nodded.

'He must have heard it from Mrs Luxmore. Easy enough to get the story out of her. That sort of thing would have amused him.'

'It might have been a dangerous story – to you – in the hands of a man like Shaitana.'

Despard shrugged his shoulders.

'I wasn't afraid of Shaitana.'

Poirot didn't answer.

Despard said quietly:

'That again you have to take my word for. It's true enough, I suppose, that I had a kind of motive for Shaitana's death. Well, the truth's out now – take it or leave it.'

Poirot held out a hand.

'I will take it, Major Despard. I have no doubt at all that things in South America happened exactly as you have described.'

Despard's face lit up.

'Thanks,' he said laconically.

And he clasped Poirot's hand warmly.

CHAPTER TWENTY-TWO

Evidence from Combeacre

Superintendent Battle was in the police station of Combeacre.

Inspector Harper, rather red in the face, talked in a slow, pleasing Devonshire voice.

'That's how it was, sir. Seemed all as right as rain. The doctor was satisfied. Everyone was satisfied. Why not?'

'Just give me the facts about the two bottles again. I want to get it quite clear.'

'Syrup of Figs – that's what the bottle was. She took it regular, it seems. Then there was this hat paint she'd been using – or rather the young lady, her companion, had been using for her. Brightening up a garden hat. There was a good deal left over, and the bottle broke, and Mrs Benson herself said, "Put it in that old bottle – the Syrup of Figs bottle." That's all right. The servants heard her. The young lady, Miss Meredith, and the housemaid and the parlour-maid – they all agree on that. The paint was put into the old Syrup of Figs bottle and it was put up on the top shelf in the bathroom with other odds and ends.'

'Not re-labelled?'

'No. Careless, of course; the coroner commented on that.'

'Go on.'

'On this particular night the deceased went into the bathroom, took down a Syrup of Figs bottle, poured herself out a good dose and drank it. Realized what she'd done and they sent off at once for the doctor. He was out on a case, and it was some time before they could get at him. They did all they could, but she died.'

'She herself believed it to be an accident?'

'Oh, yes – everyone thought so. It seems clear the bottles must have got mixed up somehow. It was suggested the housemaid did it when she dusted, but she swears she didn't.'

Superintendent Battle was silent – thinking. Such an easy business. A bottle taken down from an upper shelf, put in place of the other. So difficult to trace a mistake like that to its source. Handled with gloves, possibly, and anyway, the last prints would be those of Mrs Benson herself. Yes, so easy – so simple. But, all the same, murder! The perfect crime.

But why? That still puzzled him – why?

'This young lady-companion, this Miss Meredith, she didn't come into money at Mrs Benson's death?' he asked.

Inspector Harper shook his head.

No. She'd only been there about six weeks. Difficult place, I should imagine. Young ladies didn't stay long as a rule.'

Battle was still puzzled. Young ladies didn't stay long. A difficult woman, evidently. But if Anne Meredith had been unhappy, she could have left as her predecessors had done. No need to kill – unless it were sheer unreasoning vindictiveness. He shook his head. That suggestion did not ring true.

'Who did get Mrs Benson's money?'

'I couldn't say, sir, nephews and nieces, I believe. But it wouldn't be very much – not when it was divided up, and I heard as how most of her income was one of these annuities.'

Nothing there then. But Mrs Benson had died. And Anne Meredith had not told him that she had been at Combeacre.

It was all profoundly unsatisfactory.

He made diligent and painstaking inquiries. The doctor was quite clear and emphatic. No reason to believe it was anything but an accident. Miss – couldn't remember her name – nice girl but rather helpless – had been very upset and distressed. There was the vicar. He remembered Mrs Benson's last companion – a nice modest-looking girl. Always came to church with Mrs Benson. Mrs Benson had been – not difficult – but a trifle severe towards young people. She was the rigid type of Christian.

Battle tried one or two other people but learned nothing of value. Anne Meredith was hardly remembered. She had lived among them a few months – that was all – and her personality was not sufficiently vivid to make a lasting impression. A nice little thing seemed to be the accepted description.

Mrs Benson loomed out a little more clearly. A self-righteous grenadier of a woman, working her companions hard and changing her servants often. A disagreeable woman – but that was all.

Nevertheless Superintendent Battle left Devonshire under the firm impression that, for some reason unknown, Anne Meredith had deliberately murdered her employer.

CHAPTER TWENTY-THREE

The Evidence of a Pair of Silk Stockings

As Superintendent Battle's train rushed eastwards through England, Anne Meredith and Rhoda Dawes were in Hercule Poirot's sitting-room.

Anne had been unwilling to accept the invitation that had reached her by the morning's post, but Rhoda's counsel had prevailed.

'Anne – you're a coward – yes, a coward. It's no good going on being an ostrich, burying your head in the sand. There's been a murder and you're one of the suspects – the least likely one perhaps –'

'That would be the worst,' said Anne with a touch of humour. 'It's always the least likely person who did it.'

'But you are one,' continued Rhoda, undisturbed by the interruption. 'And it's no use putting your nose in the air as though murder was a nasty smell and nothing to do with you.'

'It *is* nothing to do with me,' Anne persisted. 'I mean, I'm quite willing to answer any questions the police want to ask me, but this man, this Hercule Poirot, he's an outsider.'

'And what will he think if you hedge and try to get out of it? He'll think you're bursting with guilt.'

'I'm certainly not bursting with guilt,' said Anne coldly.

'Darling, I know that. You couldn't murder anybody if you tried. But horrible suspicious foreigners don't know that. I think we ought to go nicely to his house. Otherwise he'll come down here and try to worm things out of the servants.'

'We haven't got any servants.'

'We've got Mother Astwell. She can wag a tongue with

171

anybody! Come on, Anne, let's go. It will be rather fun really.'

'I don't see why he wants to see me.' Anne was obstinate.

'To put one over on the official police, of course,' said Rhoda impatiently. 'They always do – the amateurs, I mean. They make out that Scotland Yard are all boots and brainlessness.'

'Do you think this man Poirot is clever?'

'He doesn't look a Sherlock,' said Rhoda. 'I expect he has been quite good in his day. He's gaga now, of course. He must be at least sixty. Oh, come on, Anne, let's go and see the old boy. He may tell us dreadful things about the others.'

'All right,' said Anne, and added, 'You do *enjoy* all this so, Rhoda.'

'I suppose because it isn't my funeral,' said Rhoda. 'You were a noodle, Anne, not just to have looked up at the right minute. If only you had, you could live like a duchess for the rest of your life on blackmail.'

So it came about that at three o'clock of that same afternoon, Rhoda Dawes and Anne Meredith sat primly on their chairs in Poirot's neat room and sipped blackberry *sirop* (which they disliked very much but were too polite to refuse) from old-fashioned glasses.

'It was most amiable of you to accede to my request, mademoiselle,' Poirot was saying.

'I'm sure I shall be glad to help in any way I can,' murmured Anne vaguely.

'It is a little matter of memory.'

'Memory?'

'Yes, I have already put these questions to Mrs Lorrimer, to Dr Roberts and to Major Despard. None of them, alas, have given me the response that I hoped for.'

Anne continued to look at him inquiringly.

'I want you, mademoiselle, to cast your mind back to that evening in the drawing-room of Mr Shaitana.'

A weary shadow passed over Anne's face. Was she never to be free of that nightmare?'

Poirot noticed the expression.

'*C'est pénible, n'est ce pas?* That is very natural. You, so young as you are, to be brought in contact with horror for the first time. Probably you have never known or seen a violent death.'

Rhoda's feet shifted a little uncomfortably on the floor.

'Well?' said Anne

'Cast your mind back. I want you to tell me what you remember of that room?'

Anne stared at him suspiciously.

'I don't understand?'

'But yes. The chairs, the tables, the ornaments, the wall-paper, the curtains, the fire-irons. You saw them all. Can you not then describe them?'

'Oh, I see.' Anne hesitated, frowning. 'It's difficult. I don't really think I remember. I couldn't say what the wallpaper was like. I think the walls were painted – some inconspicuous colour. There were rugs on the floor. There was a piano.' She shook her head. 'I really couldn't tell you any more.'

'But you are not trying, mademoiselle. You must re-member some object, some ornament, some piece of bric-à-brac?'

'There was a case of Egyptian jewellery, I remember,' said Anne slowly. 'Over by the window.'

'Oh, yes, at the extreme other end of the room from the table on which lay the little dagger.'

Anne looked at him.

'I never heard which table that was on.'

'*Pas si bête*,' commented Poirot to himself. 'But then, no more is Hercule Poirot! If she knew me better she would realize I would never lay a *piège* as gross as that!'

Aloud he said:

'A case of Egyptian jewellery, you say?'

Anne answered with some enthusiasm.

'Yes – some of it was lovely. Blues and red. Enamel. One or two lovely rings. And scarabs – but I don't like them so much.'

'He was a great collector, Mr Shaitana,' murmured Poirot.

'Yes, he must have been,' Anne agreed. 'The room was full of stuff. One couldn't begin to look at it all.'

'So that you cannot mention anything else that particularly struck your notice?'

Anne smiled a little as she said:

'Only a vase of chrysanthemums that badly wanted their water changed.'

'Ah, yes, servants are not always too particular about that.'

Poirot was silent for a moment or two.

Anne asked timidly.

'I'm afraid I didn't notice – whatever it is you wanted me to notice.'

Poirot smiled kindly.

'It does not matter, *mon enfant*. It was, indeed, an outside chance. Tell me, have you seen the good Major Despard lately?'

He saw the delicate pink colour come up in the girl's face. She replied:

'He said he would come and see us again quite soon.'

Rhoda said impetuously:

'*He* didn't do it, anyway! Anne and I are quite sure of that.'

Poirot twinkled at them.

'How fortunate – to have convinced two such charming young ladies of one's innocence.'

'Oh, dear,' thought Rhoda. 'He's going to be French, and it does embarrass me so.'

She got up and began examining some etchings on the wall.

'These are awfully good,' she said.

'They are not bad,' said Poirot.

He hesitated, looking at Anne.

'Mademoiselle,' he said at last. 'I wonder if I might ask you to do me a great favour – oh, nothing to do with the murder. This is an entirely private and personal matter.'

Anne looked a little surprised. Poirot went on speaking in a slightly embarrassed manner.

'It is, you understand, that Christmas is coming on. I have to buy presents for many nieces and grand-nieces. And it is a little difficult to choose what young ladies like in this present time. My tastes, alas, are rather old-fashioned.'

'Yes?' said Anne kindly.

'Silk stockings, now – are silk stockings a welcome present to receive?'

'Yes, indeed. It's always nice to be given stockings.'

'You relieve my mind. I will ask my favour. I have obtained some different colours. There are, I think, about fifteen or sixteen pairs. Would you be so amiable as to look through them and set aside half a dozen pairs that seem to you the most desirable?'

'Certainly I will,' said Anne, rising, with a laugh.

Poirot directed her towards a table in an alcove – a table whose contents were strangely at variance, had she but known it, with the well-known order and neatness of Hercule Poirot. There were stockings piled up in untidy heaps – some fur-lined gloves – calendars and boxes of bonbons.

'I send off my parcels very much *à l'avance*,' Poirot explained. 'See, mademoiselle, here are the stockings. Select me, I pray of you, six pairs.'

He turned, intercepting Rhoda, who was following him.

'As for mademoiselle here, I have a little treat for her – a treat that would be no treat to you, I fancy, Mademoiselle Meredith.'

'What is it?' cried Rhoda.

He lowered his voice.

'A knife, mademoiselle, with which twelve people once stabbed a man. It was given to me as a souvenir by the Compagnie Internationale des Wagons Lits.'

'Horrible,' cried Anne.

'Ooh! Let me see,' said Rhoda.

Poirot led her through into the other room, talking as he went.

'It was given me by the Compagnie Internationale des Wagons Lits because –'

They passed out of the room.

They returned three minutes later. Anne came towards them.

'I think these six are the nicest, M. Poirot. Both these are very good evening shades, and this lighter colour would be nice when summer comes and it's daylight in the evening.'

'*Mille remerciments, mademoiselle.*'

He offered them more *sirop*, which they refused, and finally accompanied them to the door, still talking genially.

When they had finally departed he returned to the room and went straight to the littered table. The pile of stockings still lay in a confused heap. Poirot counted the six selected pairs and then went on to count the others.

He had bought nineteen pairs. There were now only seventeen.

He nodded his head slowly.

CHAPTER TWENTY-FOUR

Elimination of Three Murderers?

On arrival in London, Superintendent Battle came straight to Poirot. Anne and Rhoda had then been gone an hour or more.

Without more ado, the superintendent recounted the result of his researches in Devonshire.

'We're on to it – not a doubt of it,' he finished. 'That's what Shaitana was aiming at – with his "domestic accident" business. But what gets me is the motive. Why did she want to kill the woman?'

'I think I can help you there, my friend.'

'Go ahead, M. Poirot.'

'This afternoon I conducted a little experiment. I induced mademoiselle and her friend to come here. I put to them my usual questions as to what there was in the room that night.'

Battle looked at him curiously.

'You're very keen on that question.'

'Yes, it's useful. It tells me a good deal. Mademoiselle Meredith was suspicious – very suspicious. She takes nothing for granted, that young lady. So that good dog, Hercule Poirot, he does one of his best tricks. He lays a clumsy amateurish trap. Mademoiselle mentions a case of jewellery. I say was not that at the opposite end of the room from the table with the dagger. Mademoiselle does not fall into the trap. She avoids it cleverly. And after that she is pleased with herself, and her vigilance relaxes. So that is the object of this visit – to get her to admit that she knew where the dagger was, and that she noticed it! Her spirits rise when she has, as she thinks, defeated me. She talked quite freely about the jewellery. She has noticed many details of it.

There is nothing else in the room that she remembers – except that a vase of chrysanthemums needed its water changing.'

'Well?' said Battle.

'Well, it is significant, that. Suppose we knew nothing about this girl. Her word would give us a clue to her character. She notices flowers. She is, then, fond of flowers? No, since she does not mention a very big bowl of early tulips which would at once have attracted the attention of a flower lover. No, it is the paid companion who speaks – the girl whose duty it has been to put fresh water in the vases – and, allied to that, there is a girl who loves and notices jewellery. Is not that, at least, suggestive?'

'Ah,' said Battle. 'I'm beginning to see what you're driving at.'

'Precisely. As I told you the other day, I place my cards on the table. When you recounted her history the other day, and Mrs Oliver made her startling announcement, my mind went at once to an important point. The murder could not have been committed for gain, since Miss Meredith had still to earn her living after it happened. Why, then? I considered Miss Meredith's temperament as it appeared superficially. A rather timid young girl, poor, but well-dressed, fond of pretty things. . . . The temperament, is it not, of a *thief*, rather than a murderer. And I asked immediately if Mrs Eldon had been a tidy woman. You replied that no, she had not been tidy. I formed a hypothesis. Supposing that Anne Meredith was a girl with a weak streak in her character – the kind of girl who takes little things from the big shops. Supposing that, poor, and yet loving pretty things, she helped herself once or twice to things from her employer. A brooch, perhaps, an odd half-crown or two, a string of beads. Mrs Eldon, careless, untidy, would put down these disappearances to her own carelessness. She would not suspect her gentle little mother's-help. But, now, suppose a different type of employer – an employer who *did* notice – accused Anne Meredith of theft. That would be a possible motive for murder. As I said the other evening, Miss Meredith would only commit a murder through fear. She knows that her employer will be able to prove the theft. There is only one thing that can save her: her employer must die. And so she changes the bottles, and Mrs Benson dies – ironically enough convinced that the mistake is her own, and not suspecting for a minute that the cowed, frightened girl has had a hand in it.'

'It's possible,' said Superintendent Battle. 'It's only a hypothesis, but it's possible.'

'It is a little more than possible, my friend – it is also probable. For this afternoon I laid a little trap nicely baited – the real trap – after the sham one had been circumvented. If what I suspect is true, Anne Meredith will never, never be able to resist a really expensive pair of stockings! I ask her to aid me. I let her know carefully that I am not sure exactly how many stockings there are, I go out of the room, leaving her alone – and the result, my friend, is that I have now seventeen pairs of stockings, instead of nineteen, and that two pairs have gone away in Anne Meredith's handbag.'

'Whew!' Superintendent Battle whistled. 'What a risk to take, though.'

'*Pas du tout.* What does she think I suspect her of? Murder. What is the risk, then, in stealing a pair, or two pairs, of silk stockings? I am not looking for a thief. And, besides, the thief, or the kleptomaniac, is always the same – convinced that she can get away with it.'

Battle nodded his head.

'That's true enough. Incredibly stupid. The pitcher goes to the well time after time. Well, I think between us we've arrived fairly clearly at the truth. Anne Meredith was caught stealing. Anne Meredith changed a bottle from one shelf to another. We know that was murder – but I'm damned if we could ever prove it. Successful crime No. 2.

Roberts gets away with it. Anne Meredith gets away with it. But what about Shaitana? Did Anne Meredith kill Shaitana?'

He remained silent for a moment or two, then he shook his head.

'It doesn't work out right,' he said reluctantly. 'She's not one to take a risk. Change a couple of bottles, yes. She knew no one could fasten that on her. It was absolutely safe – because anyone might have done it! Of course, it mightn't have worked. Mrs Benson might have noticed before she drank the stuff, or she mightn't have died from it. It was what I call a *hopeful* kind of murder. It might work or it mightn't. Actually, it did. But Shaitana was a very different pair of shoes. That was deliberate, audacious, purposeful murder.'

Poirot nodded his head.

'I agree with you. The two types of crime are not the same.'

Battle rubbed his nose.

'So that seems to wipe her out as far as he's concerned. Roberts and the girl, both crossed off our list. What about Despard? Any luck with the Luxmore woman?'

Poirot narrated his adventures of the preceding afternoon.

Battle grinned.

'I know that type. You can't disentangle what they remember from what they invent.'

Poirot went on. He described Despard's visit, and the story the latter had told.

'Believe him?' Battle asked abruptly.

'Yes, I do.'

Battle sighed.

'So do I. Not the type to shoot a man because he wanted the man's wife. Anyway, what's wrong with the divorce court? Everyone flocks there. And he's not a professional man; it wouldn't ruin him, or anything like that. No, I'm of the opinion that our late lamented Mr Shaitana struck a snag there. Murderer No. 3. wasn't a murderer, after all.'

He looked at Poirot.

'That leaves —'

'Mrs Lorrimer,' said Poirot.

The telephone rang. Poirot got up and answered it. He spoke a few words, waited, spoke again. Then he hung up the receiver and returned to Battle.

His face was very grave.

'That was Mrs Lorrimer speaking,' he said. 'She wants me to come round and see her — now.'

He and Battle looked at each other. The latter shook his head slowly.

'Am I wrong?' he said. 'Or were you expecting something of the kind?'

'I wondered,' said Hercule Poirot. 'That was all. I wondered.'

'You'd better get along,' said Battle. 'Perhaps you'll manage to get at the truth at last.'

CHAPTER TWENTY-FIVE

Mrs Lorrimer Speaks

The day was not a bright one, and Mrs Lorrimer's room seemed rather dark and cheerless. She herself had a grey look, and seemed much older than she had done on the occasion of Poirot's last visit.

She greeted him with her usual smiling assurance.

'It is very nice of you to come so promptly, M. Poirot. You are a busy man, I know.'

'At your service, madame,' said Poirot with a little bow.

Mrs Lorrimer pressed the bell by the fireplace.

'We will have tea brought in. I don't know what you feel about it, but I always think it's a mistake to rush straight into confidences without any decent paving of the way.'

'There are to be confidences, then, madame?'

Mrs Lorrimer did not answer, for at that moment her maid answered the bell. When she had received the order and gone again, Mrs Lorrimer said dryly:

'You said, if you remember, when you were last here, that you would come if I sent for you. You had an idea, I think, of the reason that should prompt me to send.'

There was no more just then. Tea was brought. Mrs Lorrimer dispensed it, talking intelligently on various topics of the day.

Taking advantage of a pause, Poirot remarked:

'I hear you and little Mademoiselle Meredith had tea together the other day.'

'We did. Have you seen her lately?'

'This very afternoon.'

'She is in London, then, or have you been down to Wallingford?'

'No. She and her friend were so amiable as to pay me a visit.'

'Ah, the friend. I have not met her.'

Poirot said, smiling a little:

'This murder – it has made for me a *rapprochement*. You and Mademoiselle Meredith have tea together. Major Despard, he, too, cultivates Miss Meredith's acquaintance. The Dr Roberts, he is perhaps the only one out of it.'

'I saw him out at bridge the other day,' said Mrs Lorrimer. 'He seemed quite his usual cheerful self.'

'As fond of bridge as ever?'

'Yes – still making the most outrageous bids – and very often getting away with it.'

She was silent for a moment or two, then said:

'Have you seen Superintendent Battle lately?'

'Also this afternoon. He was with me when you telephoned.'

Shading her face from the fire with one hand, Mrs Lorrimer asked:

'How is he getting on?'

Poirot said gravely:

'He is not very rapid, the good Battle. He gets there slowly, but he does get there in the end, madame.'

'I wonder.' Her lips curved in a faintly ironical smile.

She went on:

'He has paid me quite a lot of attention. He has delved, I think, into my past history right back to my girlhood. He has interviewed my friends, and chatted to my servants – the ones I have now and the ones who have been with me in former years. What he hoped to find I do not know, but he certainly did not find it. He might as well have accepted what I told him. It was the truth. I knew Mr Shaitana very slightly. I met him at Luxor, as I said, and our acquaintanceship was never more than an acquaintanceship. Superintendent Battle will not be able to get away from these facts.'

'Perhaps not,' said Poirot.

'And you, M. Poirot? Have not you made any inquiries?'

'About you, madame?'

'That is what I meant.'

Slowly the little man shook his head.

'It would have been to no avail.'

'Just exactly what do you mean by that, M. Poirot?'

'I will be quite frank, madame. I have realized from the beginning that, of the four persons in Mr Shaitana's room that night, the one with the best brains, with the coolest, most logical head, was you, madame. If I had to lay money on the chance of one of those four planning a murder and getting away with it successfully, it is on you that I should place my money.'

Mrs Lorrimer's brows rose.

'Am I expected to feel flattered?' she asked drily.

Poirot went on, without paying any attention to her interruption:

'For a crime to be successful, it is usually necessary to think every detail of it out beforehand. All possible contingencies must be taken into account. The *timing* must be accurate. The *placing* must be scrupulously correct. Dr Roberts might bungle a crime through haste and over-confidence; Major Despard would probably be too prudent to commit one; Miss Meredith might lose her head and give herself away. You, madame, would do none of these things. You would be clear-headed and cool, you are sufficiently resolute of character, and could be sufficiently obsessed with an idea to the extent of overruling prudence, you are not the kind of woman to lose her head.'

Mrs Lorrimer sat silent for a minute or two, a curious smile playing round her lips. At last she said:

'So that is what you think of me, M. Poirot. That I am the kind of woman to commit an ideal murder.'

'At least you have the amiability not to resent the idea.'

'I find it very interesting. So it is your idea that I am the only person who could successfully have murdered Shaitana?'

Poirot said slowly:

'There is a difficulty there, madame.'

'Really? Do tell me.'

'You may have noticed that I said just now a phrase something like this: "For a crime to be successful it is usually necessary to plan every detail of it carefully beforehand." "Usually" is the word to which I want to draw your attention. For there *is* another type of successful crime. Have you ever said suddenly to any one, "Throw a stone and see if you can hit that tree," and the person obeys quickly, without thinking – and surprisingly often he *does* hit the tree? But when he comes to repeat the throw it is not so easy – for he has begun to *think*. 'So hard – no harder – a little more to the right – to the left.' The first was an almost unconscious action, the body obeying the mind as the body of an animal does. *Eh bien*, madame, there is a type of crime like that, a crime committed on the spur of the moment – an inspiration – a flash of genius – without time to pause or think. And that, madame, was the kind of crime that killed Mr Shaitana. A sudden dire necessity, a flash of inspiration, rapid execution.'

He shook his head.

'And that, madame, is not your type of crime at all. If you killed Mr Shaitana, it should have been a premeditated crime.'

'I see.' Her hand waved softly to and fro, keeping the heat of the fire from her face. 'And, of course, it wasn't a premeditated crime, so I couldn't have killed him – eh, M. Poirot?'

Poirot bowed.

'That is right, madame.'

'And yet –' She leaned forward, her waving hand stopped. *'I did kill Shaitana, M. Poirot . . .'*

CHAPTER TWENTY-SIX

The Truth

There was a pause – a very long pause.

The room was growing dark. The firelight leaped and flickered.

Mrs Lorrimer and Hercule Poirot looked not at each other, but at the fire. It was as though time was momentarily in abeyance.

Then Hercule Poirot sighed and stirred.

'So it was that – all the time . . . *Why* did you kill him, madame?'

'I think you know why, M. Poirot.'

'Because he knew something about you – something that had happened long ago?'

'Yes.'

'And that something was – another death, madame?'

She bowed her head.

Poirot said gently:

'Why did you tell me? What made you send for me today?'

'You told me once that I should do so some day.'

'Yes – that is, I hoped . . . I knew, madame, that there was only one way of learning the truth as far as you were concerned – and that was by your own free will. If you did not choose to speak, you would not do so, and you would never give yourself away. But there was a chance – that you yourself might *wish* to speak.'

Mrs Lorrimer nodded.

'It was clever of you to foresee that – the weariness – the loneliness –'

Her voice died away.

Poirot looked at her curiously.

'So it has been like that? Yes, I can understand it might be . . .'

'Alone – quite alone,' said Mrs Lorrimer. 'No one knows what that means unless they have lived, as I have lived, with the knowledge of what one has done.'

Poirot said gently:

'Is it an impertinence, madame, or may I be permitted to offer my sympathy?'

She bent her head a little.

'Thank you, M. Poirot.'

There was another pause, then Poirot said, speaking in a slightly brisker tone:

'Am I to understand, madame, that you took the words Mr Shaitana spoke at dinner as a direct menace aimed at you?'

She nodded.

'I realized at once that he was speaking so that one person should understand him. That person was myself. The reference to a woman's weapon being poison was meant for me. He *knew*. I had suspected it once before. He had brought the conversation round to a certain famous trial, and I saw his eyes watching me. There was a kind of uncanny knowledge in them. But, of course, that night I was quite sure.'

'And you were sure, too, of his future intentions?'

Mrs Lorrimer said drily:

'It was hardly likely that the presence of Superintendent Battle and yourself was an accident. I took it that Shaitana was going to advertise his own cleverness by pointing out to you both that he had discovered something that no one else had suspected.'

'How soon did you make up your mind to act, madame?'

Mrs Lorrimer hesitated a little.

'It is difficult to remember exactly when the idea came into my mind,' she said. 'I had noticed the dagger before

187

going into dinner. When we returned to the drawing-room I picked it up and slipped it into my sleeve. No one saw me do it. I made sure of that.'

'It would be dexterously done, I have no doubt, madame.'

'I made up my mind then exactly what I was going to do. I had only to carry it out. It was risky, perhaps, but I considered that it was worth trying.'

'That is your coolness, your successful weighing of chances, coming into play. Yes, I see that.'

'We started to play bridge,' continued Mrs Lorrimer. Her voice cool and unemotional. 'At last an opportunity arose. I was dummy. I strolled across the room to the fireplace. Shaitana had dozed off to sleep. I looked over at the others. They were all intent on the game. I leant over and – and did it –'

Her voice shook just a little, but instantly it regained its cool aloofness.

'I spoke to him. It came into my head that that would make a kind of alibi for me. I made some remark about the fire, and then pretended he had answered me and went on again, saying something like: "I agree with you. I do not like radiators, either."'

'He did not cry out at all?'

'No. I think he made a little grunt – that was all. It might have been taken for words from a distance.'

'And then?'

'And then I went back to the bridge table. The last trick was just being played.'

'And you sat down and resumed play?'

'Yes.'

'With sufficient interest in the game to be able to tell me nearly all the calling and the hands two days later?'

'Yes,' said Mrs Lorrimer simply.

'*Epatant!*' said Hercule Poirot.

He leaned back in his chair. He nodded his head several times. Then, by way of a change, he shook it.

'But there is still something, madame, that I do not understand.'

'Yes?'

'It seems to me that there is some factor that I have missed. You are a woman who considers and weighs everything carefully. You decide that, for a certain reason, you will run an enormous risk. You do run it – successfully. And then, not two weeks later, you change your mind. Frankly, madame, that does not seem to me to ring true.'

A queer little smile twisted her lips.

'You are quite right, M. Poirot, there is one factor that you do not know. Did Miss Meredith tell you where she met me the other day?'

'It was, I think she said, near Mrs Oliver's flat.'

'I believe that is so. But I meant the actual name of the street. Anne Meredith met me in Harley Street.'

'Ah!' He looked at her attentively. 'I begin to see.'

'Yes, I thought you would. I had been to see a specialist there. He told me what I already half suspected.'

Her smile widened. It was no longer twisted and bitter. It was suddenly sweet.

'I shall not play very much more bridge, M. Poirot. Oh, he didn't say so in so many words. He wrapped up the truth a little. With great care, etc., etc., I might live several years. But I shall not take any great care. I am not that kind of a woman.'

'Yes, yes, I begin to understand,' said Poirot.

'It made a difference, you see. A month – two months, perhaps – not more. And then, just as I left the specialist, I met Miss Meredith. I asked her to have tea with me.'

She paused, then went on:

'I am not, after all, a wholly wicked woman. All the time we were having tea I was thinking. By my action the other evening I had not only deprived the man Shaitana of life (that was done, and could not be undone), I had also, to a varying degree, affected unfavourably the lives of three

189

other people. Because of what I had done, Dr Roberts, Major Despard and Anne Meredith, none of whom had injured me in any way, were passing through a very grave ordeal, and might even be in danger. That, at least, I could undo. I don't know that I felt particularly moved by the plight of either Dr Roberts or Major Despard – although both of them had presumably a much longer span of life in front of them than I had. They were men, and could, to a certain extent, look after themselves. But when I looked at Anne Meredith –'

She hesitated, then continued slowly:

'Anne Meredith was only a girl. She had the whole of her life in front of her. This miserable business might ruin that life . . .

'I didn't like the thought of that . . .

'And then, M. Poirot, with these ideas growing in my mind, I realized that what you had hinted had come true. I was not going to be able to keep silence. This afternoon I rang you up . . .'

Minutes passed.

Hercule Poirot leaned forward. He stared, deliberately stared through the gathering gloom, at Mrs Lorrimer. She returned that intent gaze quietly and without any nervousness.

He said at last:

'Mrs Lorrimer, are you sure – are you *positive* (you will tell me the truth, will you not?) – *that the murder of Mr Shaitana was not premeditated*? Is it not a fact that you planned the crime *beforehand* – that you went to that dinner with the murder already mapped out in your mind?'

Mrs Lorrimer stared at him for a moment, then she shook her head sharply.

'No,' she said.

'You did not plan the murder beforehand?'

'Certainly not.'

'Then – then . . . Oh, you are lying to me – you must be lying! . . .'

Mrs Lorrimer's voice cut into the air like ice.

'Really, M. Poirot, you forget yourself.'

The little man sprang to his feet. He paced up and down the room, muttering to himself, uttering ejaculations.

Suddenly he said:

'Permit me.'

And, going to the switch, he turned on the electric lights.

He came back, sat down in his chair, placed both hands on his knees and stared straight at his hostess.

'The question is,' he said, 'can Hercule Poirot possibly be wrong?'

'No one can always be right,' said Mrs Lorrimer coldly.

'I am,' said Poirot. 'Always I am right. It is so invariable that it startles me. But now it looks, it very much looks, as though I am wrong. And that upsets me. Presumably, you know what you are saying. It is your murder! Fantastic, then, that Hercule Poirot should know better than you do how you committed it.'

'Fantastic and very absurd,' said Mrs Lorrimer still more coldly.

'I am, then, mad. Decidedly I am mad: No – *sacré nom d'un petit bonhomme* – I am *not* mad! I am right. I *must* be right. I am willing to believe that you killed Mr Shaitana – *but you cannot have killed him in the way you say you did*. No one can do a thing that is not *dans son charactère!*'

He paused. Mrs Lorrimer drew in an angry breath and bit her lips. She was about to speak, but Poirot forestalled her.

'Either the killing of Shaitana was planned beforehand – *or you did not kill him at all!*'

Mrs Lorrimer said sharply:

'I really believe you *are* mad, M. Poirot. If I am willing to admit I committed the crime, I should not be likely to lie about the way I did it. What would be the point of such a thing?'

Poirot got up again and took one turn round the room. When he came back to his seat his manner had changed. He was gentle and kindly.

'You did not kill Shaitana,' he said softly. 'I see that now. I see everything. Harley Street. And little Anne Meredith standing forlorn on the pavement. I see, too, another girl – a very long time ago, a girl who has gone through life always alone – terribly alone. Yes, I see all that. But one thing I do not see – why are you so certain that Anne Meredith did it?'

'Really, M. Poirot –'

'Absolutely useless to protest – to lie further to me, madame. *I tell you, I know the truth.* I know the very emotions that swept over you that day in Harley Street. You would not have done it for Dr Roberts – oh, no! You would not have done it for Major Despard, *non plus*. But Anne Meredith is different. You have compassion for her, *because she has done what you once did.* You do not know even – or so I imagine – what *reason* she had for the crime. But you are quite sure she did it. You were sure that first evening – the evening it happened – when Superintendent Battle invited you to give your views on the case. Yes, I know it all, you see. It is quite useless to lie further to me. You see that, do you not?'

He paused for an answer, but none came. He nodded his head in satisfaction.

'Yes, you are sensible. That is good. It is a very noble action that you perform there, madame, to take the blame on yourself and to let this child escape.'

'You forget,' said Mrs Lorrimer in a dry voice, 'I am not an innocent woman. Years ago, M. Poirot, I killed my husband . . .'

There was a moment's silence.

'I see,' said Poirot. 'It is justice. After all, only justice. You have the logical mind. You are willing to suffer for the act you committed. Murder is murder – it does not matter who the victim is. Madame, you have courage, and you have clear-sightedness. But I ask of you once more: *How can you be so sure?* How do you *know* that it was Anne Meredith who killed Mr Shaitana?'

A deep sigh broke from Mrs Lorrimer. Her last resistance had gone down before Poirot's insistence. She answered his question quite simply like a child.

'Because,' she said, 'I saw her.'

CHAPTER TWENTY-SEVEN

The Eye-Witness

Suddenly Poirot laughed. He could not help it. His head went back, and his high Gallic laugh filled the room.

'*Pardon, madame,*' he said, wiping his eyes. 'I could not help it. Here we argue and we reason! We ask questions! We invoke the psychology – and all the time *there was an eye-witness of the crime.* Tell me, I pray of you.'

'It was fairly late in the evening. Anne Meredith was dummy. She got up and looked over her partner's hand, and then she moved about the room. The hand wasn't very interesting – the conclusion was inevitable. I didn't need to concentrate on the cards. Just as we got to the last three tricks I looked over towards the fireplace. Anne Meredith was bent over Mr Shaitana. As I watched, she straightened herself – her hand had been actually on his breast – a gesture which awakened my surprise. She straightened herself, and I saw her face and her quick look over towards us. Guilt and fear – that is what I saw on her face. Of course, I didn't know what had happened then. I only wondered what on earth the girl could have been doing. Later – I knew.'

Poirot nodded.

'But *she* did not know that you knew. *She* did not know that you had seen her?'

'Poor child,' said Mrs Lorrimer. 'Young, frightened – her way to make in the world. Do you wonder that I – well, held my tongue?'

'No, no, I do not wonder.'

'Especially knowing that I – that I myself –' She finished the sentence with a shrug. 'It was certainly not my place to stand accuser. It was up to the police.'

'Quite so – but today you have gone further than that.'

Mrs Lorrimer said grimly:

'I've never been a very soft-hearted or compassionate woman, but I suppose these qualities grow upon one in one's old age. I assure you, I'm not often actuated by pity.'

'It is not always a very safe guide, madame. Mademoiselle Anne is young, she is fragile, she looks timid and frightened – oh, yes, she seems a very worthy subject for compassion. But I, *I do not agree*. Shall I tell you, madame, why Miss Anne Meredith killed Mr Shaitana. It was because he knew that she had previously killed an elderly lady to whom she was companion – because that lady had found her out in a petty theft.'

Mrs Lorrimer looked a little startled.

'Is that true, M. Poirot?'

'I have no doubt of it, whatsoever. She is so soft – so gentle – one would say. Pah! She is dangerous, madame, that little Mademoiselle Anne! Where her own safety, her own comfort, is concerned, she will strike wildly – treacherously. With Mademoiselle Anne *those two crimes will not be the end*. She will gain confidence from them. . . .'

Mrs Lorrimer said sharply:

'What you say is horrible, M. Poirot. Horrible!'

Poirot rose.

'Madame, I will now take my leave. Reflect on what I have said.'

Mrs Lorrimer was looking a little uncertain of herself. She said with an attempt at her old manner:

'If it suits me, M. Poirot, I shall deny this whole conversation. You have no witnesses, remember. What I have just told you that I saw on that fatal evening is – well, private between ourselves.'

Poirot said gravely:

'Nothing shall be done without your consent, madame. And be at peace; I have my own methods. Now that I know what I am driving at –'

He took her hand and raised it to his lips.

'Permit me to tell you, madame, that you are a most remarkable woman. All my homage and respect. Yes, indeed, a woman in a thousand. Why, you have not even done what nine hundred and ninety-nine women out of a thousand could not have resisted doing.'

'What is that?'

'Told me just why you killed your husband – and how entirely justified such a proceeding really was.'

Mrs Lorrimer drew herself up.

'Really, M. Poirot,' she said stiffly. 'My reasons were entirely my own business.'

'*Magnifique!*' said Poirot, and, once more raising her hand to his lips, he left the room.

It was cold outside the house, and he looked up and down for a taxi, but there was none in sight.

He began to walk in the direction of King's Road.

As he walked he was thinking hard. Occasionally he nodded his head; once he shook it.

He looked back over his shoulder. Some one was going up the steps of Mrs Lorrimer's house. In figure it looked very like Anne Meredith. He hesitated for a minute, wondering whether to turn back or not, but in the end he went on.

On arrival at home, he found that Battle had gone without leaving any message.

He proceeded to ring the superintendent up.

'Hallo.' Battle's voice came through. 'Got anything?'

'*Je crois bien. Mon ami*, we must get after the Meredith girl – and quickly.'

'I'm getting after her – but why quickly?'

'Because, my friend, she may be dangerous.'

Battle was silent for a minute or two. Then he said:

'I know what you mean. But there's no one . . . Oh, well, we mustn't take chances. As a matter of fact, I've written her. Official note, saying I'm calling to see her

196

tomorrow. I thought it might be a good thing to get her rattled.'

'It is a possibility, at least. I may accompany you?'

'Naturally. Honoured to have your company, M. Poirot.'

Poirot hung up the receiver with a thoughtful face.

His mind was not quite at rest. He sat for a long time in front of his fire, frowning to himself. At last, putting his fears and doubts aside, he went to bed.

'We will see in the morning,' he murmured.

But of what the morning would bring he had no idea.

CHAPTER TWENTY-EIGHT

Suicide

The summons came by telephone at the moment when Poirot was sitting down to his morning coffee and rolls.

He lifted the telephone receiver, and Battle's voice spoke:

'That M. Poirot?'

'Yes, it is. *Qu'est ce qu'il y a?*'

The mere inflection of the superintendent's voice had told him that something had happened. His own vague misgivings came back to him.

'But quickly, my friend, tell me.'

'It's Mrs Lorrimer.'

'Lorrimer – yes?'

'What the devil did you say to her – or did she say to you – yesterday? You never told me anything; in fact, you let me think that the Meredith girl was the one we were after.'

Poirot said quietly:

'What has happened?'

'Suicide.'

'Mrs Lorrimer has committed suicide?'

'That's right. It seems she has been very depressed and unlike herself lately. Her doctor had ordered her some sleeping stuff. Last night she took an overdose.'

Poirot drew a deep breath.

'There is no question of – accident?'

'Not the least. It's all cut and dried. She wrote to the three of them.'

'Which three?'

'The other three. Roberts, Despard and Miss Meredith. All fair and square – no beating about the bush. Just wrote that she would like them to know that she was taking a short-cut out of all the mess – that it was she who had killed Shaitana – and that she apologized – apologized – to all three of them for the inconvenience and annoyance they had suffered. Perfectly calm, business-like letter. Absolutely typical of the woman. She was a cool customer all right.'

For a minute or two Poirot did not answer.

So this was Mrs Lorrimer's final word. She had determined, after all, to shield Anne Meredith. A quick painless death instead of a protracted painful one, and her last action an altruistic one – the saving of the girl with whom she felt a secret bond of sympathy. The whole thing planned and carried out with quite ruthless efficiency – a suicide carefully announced to the three interested parties. What a woman! His admiration quickened. It was like her – like her clear-cut determination, her insistence on what she had decided being carried out.

He had thought to have convinced her – but evidently she had preferred her own judgement. A woman of very strong will.

Battle's voice cut into his meditations.

'What the devil did you say to her yesterday? You must have put the wind up her, and this is the result. But you implied that the result of your interview was definite suspicion of the Meredith girl.'

Poirot was silent a minute or two. He felt that, dead, Mrs Lorrimer constrained him to her will, as she could not have done if she were living.

He said at last slowly:

'I was in error . . .'

They were unaccustomed words on his tongue, and he did not like them.

'You made a mistake, eh?' said Battle. 'All the same, she must have thought you were on to her. It's a bad business – letting her slip through our fingers like this.'

'You could not have proved anything against her,' said Poirot.

'No – I suppose that's true . . . Perhaps it's all for the best. You – er – didn't mean this to happen, M. Poirot?'

Poirot's disclaimer was indignant. Then he said:

'Tell me exactly what has occurred.'

'Roberts opened his letter just before eight o'clock. He lost no time, dashed off at once in his car, leaving his parlourmaid to communicate with us, which she did. He got to the house to find that Mrs Lorrimer hadn't been called yet, rushed up to her bedroom – but it was too late. He tried artificial respiration, but there was nothing doing. Our divisional surgeon arrived soon after and confirmed his treatment.'

'What was the sleeping stuff?'

'Veronal, I think. One of the barbituric group, at any rate. There was a bottle of tablets by her bed.'

'What about the other two? Did they not try to communicate with you?'

'Despard is out of town. He hasn't had this morning's post.'

'And – Miss Meredith?'

'I've just rung her up.'

'*Eh bien?*'

'She had just opened the letter a few moments before my call came through. Post is later there.'

'What was her reaction?'

'A perfectly proper attitude. Intense relief decently veiled. Shocked and grieved – that sort of thing.'

Poirot paused a moment, then he said:

'Where are you now, my friend?'

'At Cheyne Lane.'

'*Bien.* I will come round immediately.'

In the hall at Cheyne Lane he found Dr Roberts on the point of departure. The doctor's usual florid manner was rather in abeyance this morning. He looked pale and shaken.

'Nasty business this, M. Poirot. I can't say I'm not

relieved – from my own point of view – but, to tell you the truth, it's a bit of a shock. I never really thought for a minute that it was Mrs Lorrimer who stabbed Shaitana. It's been the greatest surprise to me.'

'I, too, am surprised.'

'Quiet, well-bred, self-contained woman. Can't imagine her doing a violent thing like that. What was the motive, I wonder? Oh, well, we shall never know now. I confess I'm curious, though.'

'It must take a load off your mind – this occurrence.'

'Oh, it does, undoubtedly. It would be hypocrisy not to admit it. It's not very pleasant to have a suspicion of murder hanging over you. As for the poor woman herself – well, it was undoubtedly the best way out.'

'So she thought herself.'

Roberts nodded.

'Conscience, I suppose,' he said as he let himself out of the house.

Poirot shook his head thoughtfully. The doctor had misread the situation. It was not remorse that had made Mrs Lorrimer take her life.

On his way upstairs he paused to say a few words of comfort to the elderly parlourmaid, who was weeping quietly.

'It's so dreadful, sir. So very dreadful. We were all so fond of her. And you having tea with her yesterday so nice and quiet. And now today she's gone. I shall never forget this morning – never as long as I live. The gentleman pealing at the bell. Rang three times, he did, before I could get to it. And, "Where's your mistress?" he shot out at me. I was so flustered, I couldn't hardly answer. You see, we never went in to the mistress till she rang – that was her orders. And I just couldn't get out anything. And the doctor he says, "Where's her room?" and ran up the stairs, and me behind him, and I showed him the door, and he rushes in, not so much as knocking, and takes one look at her lying there, and, "Too late," he says. She was dead, sir. But he sent me for brandy and hot water, and he tried desperate to bring her back, but it couldn't be done. And then the police coming and all – it isn't – it isn't – decent, sir. Mrs Lorrimer wouldn't have liked it. And why the police? It's none of their business, surely, even if an accident has occurred and the poor mistress did take an overdose by mistake.'

Poirot did not reply to her question.

He said:

'Last night, was your mistress quite as usual? Did she seem upset or worried at all?'

'No, I don't think so, sir. She was tired – and I think she was in pain. She hasn't been well lately, sir.'

'No, I know.'

The sympathy in his tone made the woman go on.

'She was never one for complaining, sir, but both cook and I had been worried about her for some time. She couldn't do as much as she used to do, and things tired her. I think, perhaps, the young lady coming after you left was a bit too much for her.'

With his foot on the stairs, Poirot turned back.

'The young lady? Did a young lady come here yesterday evening?'

'Yes, sir. Just after you left, it was. Miss Meredith, her name was.'

'Did she stay long?'

'About an hour, sir.'

Poirot was silent for a minute or two, then he said:

'And afterwards?'

'The mistress went to bed. She had dinner in bed. She said she was tired.'

Again Poirot was silent; then he said:

'Do you know if your mistress wrote any letters yesterday evening?'

'Do you mean after she went to bed? I don't think so, sir.'

'But you are not sure?'

'There were some letters on the hall table ready to be posted, sir. We always took them last thing before shutting up. But I think they had been lying there since earlier in the day.'

'How many were there?'

'Two or three – I'm not quite sure, sir. Three, I think.'

'You – or cook – whoever posted them – did not happen to notice to whom they were addressed? Do not be offended at my question. It is of the utmost importance.'

'I went to the post myself with them, sir. I noticed the top one – it was to Fortnum and Mason's. I couldn't say as to the others.'

The woman's tone was earnest and sincere.

'Are you sure there were not more than three letters?'

'Yes, sir, I'm quite certain of that.'

Poirot nodded his head gravely. Once more he started up the staircase. Then he said:

'You knew, I take it, that your mistress took medicine to make her sleep?'

'Oh, yes, sir, it was the doctor's orders. Dr Lang.'

'Where was this sleeping medicine kept?'

'In the little cupboard in the mistress's room.'

Poirot did not ask any further questions. He went upstairs. His face was very grave.

On the upper landing Battle greeted him. The superintendent looked worried and harassed.

'I'm glad you've come, M. Poirot. Let me introduce you to Dr Davidson.'

The divisional surgeon shook hands. He was a tall, melancholy man.

'The luck was against us,' he said. 'An hour or two earlier, and we might have saved her.'

'H'm,' said Battle. 'I mustn't say so officially, but I'm not sorry. She was a – well, she was a lady. I don't know what her reasons were for killing Shaitana, but she may just conceivably have been justified.'

'In any case,' said Poirot, 'it is doubtful if she would have lived to stand her trial. She was a very ill woman.'

The surgeon nodded in agreement.

'I should say you were quite right. Well, perhaps it is all for the best.'

He started down the stairs.

Battle moved after him.

'One minute, doctor.'

Poirot, his hand on the bedroom door, murmured, 'I may enter – yes?'

Battle nodded over his shoulder. 'Quite all right. We're through.' Poirot passed into the room, closing the door behind him. . . .

He went over to the bed and stood looking down at the quiet, dead face.

He was very disturbed.

Had the dead woman gone to the grave in a last determined effort to save a young girl from death and disgrace – or was there a different, a more sinister explanation?

There were certain facts. . .

Suddenly he bent down, examining a dark, discoloured bruise on the dead woman's arm.

He straightened himself up again. There was a strange, cat-like gleam in his eyes that certain close associates of his would have recognized.

He left the room quickly and went downstairs. Battle and a subordinate were at the telephone. The latter laid down the receiver and said:

'He hasn't come back, sir.'

Battle said:

'Despard. I've been trying to get him. There's a letter for him with the Chelsea postmark all right.'

Poirot asked an irrelevant question.

'Had Dr Roberts had his breakfast when he came here?'

Battle stared.

'No,' he said, 'I remember he mentioned that he'd come out without it.'

'Then he will be at his house now. We can get him.'

'But why –?'

But Poirot was already busy at the dial. Then he spoke:

'Dr Roberts? It is Dr Roberts speaking? *Mais oui*, it is Poirot here. Just one question. Are you well acquainted with the handwriting of Mrs Lorrimer?'

'Mrs Lorrimer's handwriting? I – no, I don't know that I'd ever seen it before.'

'*Je vous remercie.*'

Poirot laid down the receiver quickly.

Battle was staring at him.

'What's the big idea, M. Poirot?' he asked quietly.

Poirot took him by the arm.

'Listen, my friend. A few minutes after I left this house yesterday Anne Meredith arrived. I actually saw her going up the steps, though I was not quite sure of her identity at the time. Immediately after Anne Meredith left Mrs Lorrimer went to bed. As far as the maid knows, *she did not write any letters then*. And, for reasons which you will understand when I recount to you our interview, *I do not believe that she wrote those three letters before my visit*. When did she write them, then?'

'After the servants had gone to bed?' suggested Battle. 'She got up and posted them herself.'

'That is possible, yes, but there is another possibility – *that she did not write them at all*.'

Battle whistled.

'My God, you mean –'

The telephone trilled. The sergeant picked up the receiver. He listened a minute, then turned to Battle.

'Sergeant O'Connor speaking from Despard's flat, sir. There's reason to believe that Despard's down at Wallingford-on-Thames.'

Poirot caught Battle by the arm.

'Quickly, my friend. We, too, must go to Wallingford. I tell you, I am not easy in my mind. This may not be the end. I tell you again, my friend, this young lady, she is dangerous.'

CHAPTER TWENTY-NINE

Accident

'Anne,' said Rhoda.

'Mmm?'

'No, really, Anne, don't answer with half your mind on a crossword puzzle. I want you to attend to me.'

'I am attending.'

Anne sat bolt upright and put down the paper.

'That's better. Look here, Anne.' Rhoda hesitated. 'About this man coming.'

'Superintendent Battle?'

'Yes, Anne, I wish you'd tell him – about being at the Bensons'.'

Anne's voice grew rather cold.

'Nonsense. Why should I?'

'Because – well, it might look – as though you'd been keeping something back. I'm sure it would be better to mention it.'

'I can't very well now,' said Anne coldly.

'I wish you had in the first place.'

'Well, it's too late to bother about that now.'

'Yes.' Rhoda did not sound convinced.

Anne said rather irritably:

'In any case, I can't see *why*. It's got nothing to do with all this.'

'No, of course not.'

'I was only there about two months. He only wants these things as – well – references. Two months doesn't count.'

'No, I know. I expect I'm being rather foolish, but it does worry me rather. I feel you ought to mention it. You see, if it came out some other way, it might look rather bad – your keeping dark about it, I mean.'

'I don't see how it can come out. Nobody knows but you.'

'N-no?'

Anne pounced on the slight hesitation in Rhoda's voice. 'Why, who does know?'

'Well, everyone at Combeacre,' said Rhoda after a moment's silence.

'Oh, that!' Anne dismissed it with a shrug. 'The superintendent isn't likely to come up against anyone from there. It would be an extraordinary coincidence if he did.'

'Coincidences happen.'

'Rhoda, you're being extraordinary about this. Fuss, fuss, fuss.'

'I'm terribly sorry, darling. Only you know what the police might be like if they thought you were – well – hiding things.'

'They won't know. Who's to tell them? Nobody knows but you.'

It was the second time she had said those words. At this second repetition her voice changed a little – something queer and speculative came into it.

'Oh, dear, I wish you would,' sighed Rhoda unhappily.

She looked guiltily at Anne, but Anne was not looking at her. She was sitting with a frown on her face, as though working out some calculation.

'Rather fun, Major Despard turning up,' said Rhoda.

'What? Oh, yes.'

'Anne, he *is* attractive. If you don't want him, *do, do, do* hand him over to me!'

'Don't be absurd, Rhoda. He doesn't care tuppence for me.'

'Then why does he keep on turning up? Of course he's keen on you. You're just the sort of distressed damsel that he'd enjoy rescuing. You look so beautifully helpless, Anne.'

'He's equally pleasant to both of us.'

'That's only his niceness. But if you don't want him, I

could do the sympathetic friend act – console his broken heart, etc., etc., and in the end I might get him. Who knows?' Rhoda concluded inelegantly.

'I'm sure you're quite welcome to him, my dear,' said Anne, laughing.

'He's got such a lovely back to his neck,' sighed Rhoda. 'Very brick red and muscular.'

'Darling, must you be so mawkish?'

'Do you like him, Anne?'

'Yes, very much.'

'Aren't we prim and sedate? I think he likes me a little – not as much as you, but a little.'

'Oh, but he does like you,' said Anne.

Again there was an unusual note in her voice, but Rhoda did not hear it.

'What time is our sleuth coming?' she asked.

'Twelve,' said Anne. She was silent for a minute or two, then she said, 'It's only half-past ten now. Let's go out on the river.'

'But isn't – didn't – didn't Despard say he'd come round about eleven?'

'Why should we wait in for him? We can leave a message with Mrs Astwell which way we've gone, and he can follow us along the towpath.'

'In fact, don't make yourself cheap, dear, as mother always said!' laughed Rhoda. 'Come on, then.'

She went out of the room and through the garden door. Anne followed her.

Major Despard called at Wendon Cottage about ten minutes later. He was before his time, he knew, so he was a little surprised to find both girls had already gone out.

He went through the garden and across the fields, and turned to the right along the towpath.

Mrs Astwell remained a minute or two looking after him, instead of getting on with her morning chores.

'Sweet on one or other of 'em, he is,' she observed to herself. 'I think it's Miss Anne, but I'm not certain. He don't give much away by his face. Treats 'em both alike. I'm not sure they ain't both sweet on him, too. If so, they won't be such dear friends so much longer. Nothing like a gentleman for coming between two young ladies.'

Pleasurably excited by the prospect of assisting at a budding romance, Mrs Astwell turned indoors to her task of washing up the breakfast things, when once again the door-bell rang.

'Drat that door,' said Mrs Astwell. 'Do it on purpose, they do. Parcel, I suppose. Or might be a telegram.'

She moved slowly to the front door.

Two gentlemen stood there, a small foreign gentleman and an exceedingly English, big, burly gentleman. The latter she had seen before, she remembered.

'Miss Meredith at home?' asked the big man.

Mrs Astwell shook her head.

'Just gone out.'

'Really? Which way? We didn't meet her.'

Mrs Astwell, secretly studying the amazing moustache of the other gentleman, and deciding that they looked an unlikely pair to be friends, volunteered further information.

'Gone out on the river,' she explained.

The other gentleman broke in:

'And the other lady? Miss Dawes?'

'They've both gone.'

'Ah, thank you,' said Battle. 'Let me see, which way does one get to the river?'

'First turning to the left, down the lane,' Mrs Astwell replied promptly. 'When you get to the towpath, go right. I heard them say that's the way they were going,' she added helpfully. 'Not above a quarter of an hour ago. You'll soon catch 'em up.'

'And I wonder,' she added to herself as she unwillingly closed the front door, having stared inquisitively at their retreating backs, 'who you two might be. Can't place you, somehow.'

Mrs Astwell returned to the kitchen sink, and Battle and Poirot duly took the first turning to the left – a straggling lane which soon ended abruptly at the towpath.

Poirot was hurrying along, and Battle eyed him curiously.

'Anything the matter, M. Poirot? You seem in a mighty hurry.'

'It is true. I am uneasy, my friend.'

'Anything particular?'

Poirot shook his head.

'No. But there are possibilities. You never know . . .'

'You've got something in your head,' said Battle. 'You were urgent that we should come down here this morning without losing a moment – and, my word, you made Constable Turner step on the gas! What are you afraid of? The girl's shot her bolt.'

Poirot was silent.

'What are you afraid of?' Battle repeated.

'What is one always afraid of in these cases?'

Battle nodded.

'You're quite right. I wonder –'

'You wonder what, my friend?'

Battle said slowly:

'I'm wondering if Miss Meredith knows that her friend told Mrs Oliver a certain fact.'

Poirot nodded his head in vigorous appreciation.

'Hurry, my friend,' he said.

They hastened along the river bank. There was no craft visible on the water's surface, but presently they rounded a bend, and Poirot suddenly stopped dead. Battle's quick eyes saw also.

'Major Despard,' he said.

Despard was about two hundred yards ahead of them, striding along the river bank.

A little farther on the two girls were in view in a punt on

the water, Rhoda punting – Anne lying and laughing up at her. Neither of them were looking towards the bank.

And then – *it happened*. Anne's hand outstetched, Rhoda's stagger, her plunge overboard – her desperate grasp at Anne's sleeve – the rocking boat – then an over-turned punt and two girls struggling in the water.

'See it?' cried Battle as he started to run. 'Little Meredith caught her round the ankle and tipped her in. My God, that's her fourth murder!'

They were both running hard. But some one was ahead of them. It was clear that neither girl could swim, but Despard had run quickly along the path to the nearest point, and now he plunged in and swam towards them.

'*Mon Dieu*, this is interesting,' cried Poirot. He caught Battle's arm. 'Which of them will he go for first?'

The two girls were not together. About twelve yards separated them.

Despard swam powerfully towards them – there was no check in his stroke. He was making straight for Rhoda.

Battle, in his turn, reached the nearest bank and went in. Despard had just brought Rhoda successfully to shore. He hauled her up, flung her down and plunged in again, swimming towards the spot where Anne had just gone under.

'Be careful,' called Battle. 'Weeds.'

He and Battle got to the spot at the same time, but Anne had gone under before they reached her.

They got her at last and between them towed her to the shore.

Rhoda was being ministered to by Poirot. She was sitting up now, her breath coming unevenly.

Despard and Battle laid Anne Meredith down.

'Artificial respiration,' said Battle. 'Only thing to do. But I'm afraid she's gone.'

He set to work methodically. Poirot stood by, ready to relieve him.

Despard dropped down by Rhoda.

'Are you all right?' he asked hoarsely.

She said slowly:

'You saved me. You saved *me*. . . .' She held out her hands to him, and as he took them she burst suddenly into tears.

He said, 'Rhoda . . .'

Their hands clung together . . .

He had a sudden vision – of African scrub, and Rhoda, laughing and adventurous, by his side. . . .

CHAPTER THIRTY

Murder

'Do you mean to say,' said Rhoda incredulously, 'that Anne *meant* to push me in? I know it felt like it. And she knew I can't swim. But – but was it *deliberate*?'

'It was quite deliberate,' said Poirot.

They were driving through the outskirts of London.

'But – but – why?'

Poirot did not reply for a minute or two. He thought he knew one of the motives that had led Anne to act as she had done, and that motive was sitting next to Rhoda at the minute.

Superintendent Battle coughed.

'You'll have to prepare yourself, Miss Dawes, for a bit of a shock. This Mrs Benson your friend lived with, her death wasn't quite the accident that it appeared – at least, so we've reason to suppose.'

'What do you mean?'

'We believe,' said Poirot, 'that Anne Meredith changed two bottles.'

'Oh, no – no, how horrible! It's *impossible*. Anne? Why should she?'

'She had her reasons,' said Superintendent Battle. 'But the point is, Miss Dawes, that, as far as Miss Meredith knew, *you were the only person who could give us a clue to that incident*. You didn't tell her, I suppose, that you'd mentioned it to Mrs Oliver?'

Rhoda said slowly:

'No. I thought she'd be annoyed with me.'

'She would. Very annoyed,' said Battle grimly. 'But she thought that the only danger could come from *you*, and that's why she decided to – er – eliminate you.'

'Eliminate? *Me?* Oh, how beastly! It *can't* be all true.'

'Well, she's dead now,' said Superintendent Battle, 'so we might as well leave it at that; but she wasn't a nice friend for you to have, Miss Dawes – and that's a fact.'

The car drew up in front of a door.

'We'll go in to M. Poirot's,' said Superintendent Battle, 'and have a bit of a talk about it all.'

In Poirot's sitting-room they were welcomed by Mrs Oliver, who was entertaining Dr Roberts. They were drinking sherry. Mrs Oliver was wearing one of her new horsy hats and a velvet dress with a bow on the chest on which reposed a large piece of apple core.

'Come in. Come in,' said Mrs Oliver hospitably and quite as though it were her house and not Poirot's.

'As soon as I got your telephone call I rang up Dr Roberts, and we came round here. And all his patients are dying, but he doesn't care. They're probably getting better, really. We want to hear all about everything.'

'Yes, indeed, I'm thoroughly fogged,' said Roberts.

'*Eh bien,*' said Poirot. 'The case is ended. The murderer of Mr Shaitana is found at last.'

'So Mrs Oliver told me. That pretty little thing, Anne Meredith. I can hardly believe it. A most unbelievable murderess.'

'She was a murderess all right,' said Battle. 'Three murders to her credit – and not her fault that she didn't get away with a fourth one.'

'Incredible!' murmured Roberts.

'Not at all,' said Mrs Oliver. 'Least likely person. It seems to work out in real life just the same as in books.'

'It's been an amazing day,' said Roberts. 'First Mrs Lorrimer's letter. I suppose that was a forgery, eh?'

'Precisely. A forgery written in triplicate.'

'She wrote one to herself, too?'

'Naturally. The forgery was quite skilful – it would not deceive an expert, of course – but, then, it was highly unlikely that an expert would have been called in. All the evidence pointed to Mrs Lorrimer's having committed suicide.'

'You will excuse my curiosity, M. Poirot, but what made you suspect that she had not committed suicide?'

'A little conversation that I had with a maidservant at Cheyne Lane.'

'She told you of Anne Meredith's visit the former evening?'

'That among other things. And then, you see, I had already come to a conclusion in my own mind as to the identity of the guilty person – that is, the person who killed Mr Shaitana. That person was not Mrs Lorrimer.'

'What made you suspect Miss Meredith?'

Poirot raised his hand.

'A little minute. Let me approach this matter in my own way. Let me, that is to say, eliminate. The murderer of Mr Shaitana was not Mrs Lorrimer, nor was it Major Despard, and, curiously enough, it was not Anne Meredith. . . .'

He leaned forward. His voice purred, soft and cat-like.

'You see, Dr Roberts, *you were the person who killed Mr Shaitana*; and you also killed Mrs Lorrimer . . .'

There was at least three minutes' silence. Then Roberts laughed a rather menacing laugh.

'Are you quite mad, M. Poirot? I certainly did not murder Mr Shaitana, and I could not possibly have murdered Mrs Lorrimer. My dear Battle' – he turned to the Scotland Yard man – 'are *you* standing for this?'

'I think you'd better listen to what M. Poirot has to say,' said Battle quietly.

Poirot said:

'It is true that though I have known for some time that you – and only you – could have killed Shaitana, it would not be an easy matter to prove it. But Mrs Lorrimer's case is quite different.' He leaned forward. 'It is not a case of my knowing. It is much simpler than that – for we have *an eye-witness who saw you do it*.'

216

Roberts grew very quiet. His eyes glittered. He said sharply:

'You are talking rubbish!'

'Oh, no, I am not. It was early in the morning. You bluffed your way into Mrs Lorrimer's room, where she was still heavily asleep under the influence of the drug she had taken the night before. You bluff again – pretend to see at a glance that she is dead! You pack the parlourmaid off for brandy – hot water – all the rest of it. You are left alone in the room. The maid has only had the barest peep. And then what happens?

'You may not be aware of the fact, Dr Roberts, *but certain firms of window cleaners specialize in early morning work*. A window cleaner with his ladder arrived at the same time as you did. He placed his ladder against the side of the house and began his work. The first window he tackled was that of Mrs Lorrimer's room. When, however, he saw what was going on, he quickly retired to another window, *but he had seen something first*. He shall tell us his own story.'

Poirot stepped lightly across the floor, turned a door handle, called:

'Come in, Stephens,' and returned.

A big awkward-looking man with red hair entered. In his hand he held a uniformed hat bearing the legend 'Chelsea Window Cleaners' Association' which he twirled awkwardly.

Poirot said:

'Is there anybody you recognize in this room?'

The man looked round, then gave a bashful nod of the head towards Dr Roberts.

'Him,' he said.

'Tell us when you saw him last and what he was doing.'

'This morning it was. Eight o'clock job at a lady's house in Cheyne Lane. I started on the windows there. Lady was in bed. Looked ill she did. She was just turning her head round on the pillow. This gent I took to be a doctor. He shoved her sleeve up and jabbed something into her arm about here –' He gestured. 'She just dropped back on the pillow again. I thought I'd better hop it to another window, so I did. Hope I didn't do wrong in any way?'

'You did admirably, my friend,' said Poirot.

He said quietly:

'*Eh bien*, Dr Roberts?'

'A – a simple restorative –' stammered Roberts. 'A last hope of bringing her round. It's monstrous –'

Poirot interrupted him.

'A simple restorative? – N-methyl – cyclo – hexenyl – methyl – malonyl urea,' said Poirot. He rolled out the syllables unctuously. 'Known more simply as Evipan. Used as an anaesthetic for short operations. Injected intravenously in large doses it produces instant unconsciousness. It is dangerous to use it after veronal or any barbiturates have been given. I noticed the bruised place on her arm where something had obviously been injected into a vein. A hint to the police surgeon and the drug was easily discovered by no less a person than Sir Charles Imphery, the Home Office Analyst.'

'That about cooks your goose, I think,' said Superintendent Battle. 'No need to prove the Shaitana business, though, of course, if necessary we can bring a further charge as to the murder of Mr Charles Craddock – and possibly his wife also.'

The mention of those two names finished Roberts.

He leaned back in his chair.

'I throw in my hand,' he said. 'You've got me! I suppose that sly devil Shaitana put you wise before you came that evening. And I thought I'd settled his hash so nicely.'

'It isn't Shaitana you've got to thank,' said Battle. 'The honours lie with M. Poirot here.'

He went to the door and two men entered.

Superintendent Battle's voice became official as he made the formal arrest.

As the door closed behind the accused man Mrs Oliver said happily, if not quite truthfully:

'I always *said* he did it!'

218

CHAPTER THIRTY-ONE

Cards on the Table

It was Poirot's moment, every face was turned to his in eager anticipation.

'You are very kind,' he said, smiling. 'You know, I think, that I enjoy my little lecture. I am a prosy old fellow.

'This case, to my mind, has been one of the most interesting cases I have ever come across. There was *nothing*, you see, to go upon. There were four people, one of whom *must* have committed the crime but which of the four? Was there anything to tell one? In the material sense – no. There were no tangible clues – no fingerprints – no incriminating papers or documents. There were only – the people themselves.

'And one tangible clue – the bridge scores.

'You may remember that from the beginning I showed a particular interest in those scores. They told me something about the various people who had kept them and they did more. They gave me one valuable hint. I noticed at once, in the third rubber, the figure of 1500 above the line. That figure could only represent one thing – a call of grand slam. Now if a person were to make up their minds to commit a crime under these somewhat unusual circumstances (that is, during a rubber game of bridge) that person was clearly running two serious risks. The first was that the victim might cry out and the second was that even if the victim did not cry out some one of the other three might chance to look up at the psychological moment and *actually witness the deed*.

'Now as to the first risk, nothing could be done about it. It was a matter of gambler's luck. But something could be done about the second. It stands to reason that during an interesting or an exciting hand the attention of the three players would be wholly on the game, whereas during a dull hand they were more likely to be looking about them. Now a bid of grand slam is always exciting. It is very often (as in this case it was) doubled. Every one of the three players is playing with close attention – the declarer to get his contract, the adversaries to discard correctly and to get him down. It was, then, a distinct possibility that the murder was committed during this particular hand and I determined to find out, if I could, exactly how the bidding had gone. I soon discovered that dummy during this particular hand had been Dr Roberts. I bore that in mind and approached the matter from my second angle – psychological probability. Of the four suspects Mrs Lorrimer struck me as by far the most likely to plan and carry out a successful murder – but I could not see her as committing any crime that had to be improvised on the spur of the moment. On the other hand her manner that first evening puzzled me. It suggested either that she had committed the murder herself or that she knew who had committed it. Miss Meredith, Major Despard and Dr Roberts were all psychological possibilities, though, as I have already mentioned, each of them would have committed the crime from an entirely different *angle*.

'I next made a second test. I got everyone in turn to tell me just what they remembered of the room. From that I got some very valuable information. First of all, by far the most likely person to have noticed the dagger was Dr Roberts. He was a natural observer of trifles of all kinds – what is called an observant man. Of the bridge hands, however, he remembered practically nothing at all. I did not expect him to remember much, but his complete forgetfulness looked as though he had had something else on his mind all the evening. Again, you see, Dr Roberts was indicated.

'Mrs Lorrimer I found to have a marvellous card memory, and I could well imagine that with any one of her powers of concentration a murder could easily be committed close at hand and she would never notice anything. She gave me a valuable piece of information. The grand slam was bid by Dr Roberts (quite unjustifiably) – and he bid it in her suit, not his own, so that she necessarily played the hand.

'The third test, the test on which Superintendent Battle and I built a good deal, was the discovery of the earlier murders so as to establish a similarity of method. Well, the credit for those discoveries belongs to Superintendent Battle, to Mrs Oliver and to Colonel Race. Discussing the matter with my friend Battle, he confessed himself disappointed because there were no points of similarity between any of the three earlier crimes and that of the murder of Mr Shaitana. But actually that was not true. The two murders attributed to Dr Roberts, when examined closely, *and from the psychological point of view and not the material one*, proved to be *almost exactly the same*. They, too, had been what I might describe as *public* murders. A shaving brush boldly infected in the victim's own dressing-room while the doctor officially washes his hands after a visit. The murder of Mrs Craddock under cover of a typhoid inoculation. Again done quite openly – in the sight of the world, as you might say. And the reaction of the man is the same. Pushed into a corner, he seizes a chance and acts at once – sheer bold audacious bluff – exactly like his play at bridge. As at bridge, so in the murder of Shaitana, he took a long chance and played his cards well. The blow was perfectly struck and at exactly the right moment.

'Now just at the moment that I had decided quite definitely that Dr Roberts was the man, Mrs Lorrimer asked me to come and see her – and quite convincingly accused herself of the crime! I nearly believed her! For a minute or two I *did* believe her – and then my little grey cells reasserted their mastery. It could not be – so it was not!

'But what she told me was more difficult still.

'She assured me that she had actually *seen* Anne Meredith commit the crime.

221

'It was not till the following morning – when I stood by a dead woman's bed – that I saw how I could still be right and Mrs Lorrimer still have spoken the truth.

'Anne Meredith went over to the fireplace – *and saw that Mr Shaitana was dead!* She stooped over him – perhaps stretched out her hand to the gleaming head of the jewelled pin.

'Her lips part to call out, but she does not call out. She remembers Shaitana's talk at dinner. Perhaps he had left some record. She, Anne Meredith, has a motive for desiring his death. Everyone will say that she has killed him. She dare not call out. Trembling with fear and apprehension she goes back to her seat.

'So Mrs Lorrimer is right, since she, as she thought, saw the crime committed – but I am right too, for actually she did not see it.

'If Roberts had held his hand at this point, I doubt if we could have ever brought his crimes home to him. We *might* have done so – by a mixture of bluff and various ingenious devices. I would at any rate have *tried*.

'But he lost his nerve and once again overbid his hand. And this time the cards lay wrong for him and he came down heavily.

'No doubt he was uneasy. He knew that Battle was nosing about. He foresaw the present situation going on indefinitely, the police still searching – and perhaps, by some miracle – coming on traces of his former crimes. He hit upon the brilliant idea of making Mrs Lorrimer the scapegoat for the party. His practised eye guessed, no doubt, that she was ill, and that her life could not be very much prolonged. How natural in those circumstances for her to choose a quick way out, and before taking it, confess to the crime! So he manages to get a sample of her handwriting – forges three identical letters and arrives at the house hot-foot in the morning with his story of the letter he has just received. His parlourmaid quite correctly is instructed to ring up the police. All he needs is a start. And he gets it. By the time the police surgeon arrives it is all over. Dr Roberts is ready with his story of artificial respiration that has failed. It is all perfectly plausible – perfectly straightforward.

'In all this he has no idea of throwing suspicion on Anne Meredith. He does not even know of her visit the night before. It is suicide and security only that he is aiming at.

'It is in fact an awkward moment for him when I ask if he is acquainted with Mrs Lorrimer's handwriting. If the forgery has been detected he must save himself by saying that he has never seen her handwriting. His mind works quickly, but not quickly enough.

'From Wallingford I telephone to Mrs Oliver. She plays her part by lulling his suspicions and bringing him here. And then when he is congratulating himself that all is well, though not exactly the way he has planned, the blow falls. Hercule Poirot springs! And so – the gambler will gather in no more tricks. He has thrown his cards upon the table. *C'est fini.*'

There was silence. Rhoda broke it with a sigh.

'What amazing luck that window cleaner happened to be there,' she said.

'Luck? Luck? That was not luck, mademoiselle. That was the grey cells of Hercule Poirot. And that reminds me –'

He went to the door.

'Come in – come in, my dear fellow. You acted your part *à merveille.*'

He returned accompanied by the window cleaner, who now held his red hair in his hand and who looked somehow a very different person.

'My friend Mr Gerald Hemmingway, a very promising young actor.'

'Then there was no window cleaner?' cried Rhoda. 'Nobody saw him?'

'I saw,' said Poirot. 'With the eyes of the mind one can

223

see more than with the eyes of the body. One leans back and closes the eyes –'

Despard said cheerfully:

'Let's stab him, Rhoda, and see if his ghost can come back and find out who did it.'